A
John Quinton Cord
Novel

DRAGON'S
SWORD

Betty J. Vaughn

TotalRecall Publications, Inc.
1103 Middlecreek
Friendswood, Texas 77546
281-992-3131 TEL
www.totalrecallpress.com

ISBN: 978-1-59095-380-8
UPC: 6-43977-23800-9
Library of Congress Control Number: 2019936624

Printed in the United States of America with simultaneous printings in Australia, Canada, and United Kingdom.

FIRST EDITION
1 2 3 4 5 6 7 8 9 10

I would like to give special thanks to my editor and life-long friend, Dr. Judith Conway Gordon, and to my husband, James Martin Atwater, who read each chapter as I finished, making corrections and suggestions that were a material contribution to the plot line.

About the Author

Betty J. Vaughn, former department chair and art teacher at Enloe Magnet High School in Raleigh, NC, following years of teaching, launched a career as an author.

A prize-winning visual artist with paintings in collections worldwide, Mrs. Vaughn designed the magnet art program at Enloe where her students consistently won top honors. The recipient of a three-year Federal Grant to the Wake County School System, she led Enloe Enterprises, Inc. in operating an art gallery, a summer arts camp, and an Emmy award winning television production company. As a result of the Enterprises Enloe was selected as one of the ten best art schools in the nation by Business Week Magazine. She wrote and published a monthly newsletter for the Enterprises and is the author of numerous professional articles.

Betty loves to travel and led study tours of Europe for many years. History, art, and books are a lifelong passion. Both as a teacher of advanced placement art history and as a writer, Mrs. Vaughn brings the story of the past alive through the people who lived it. The Quint Cord series focuses on the issues currently facing us as a people and country.

Editors Comments

"I recently had the pleasure of reading Betty J. Vaughn's book, Dragon's Sword. It is her second book in the Quint Cord series.

It is replete with international intrigue, political mayhem, and counterintelligence attempts to thwart an enemy to world peace. This gifted author, is adept at creating nail-biting thrillers that sustain excitement and reader interest from cover-to-cover.

Her latest book, *Dragon's Sword*, is sure to keep the reader in suspense with a carefully crafted plot and clearly delineated interrelationships between characters. Will Quint Cord, CIA operative, thwart the efforts of a demonic, elusive hacker, or will he and his hacker girlfriend fail in their attempts to stop this ruthless computer expert from gaining control of the world stage through his GPS satellite-implanted virus?

This action-packed, timely book, so relative to looming threats in today's international arena, is a "must-read."

I read this book in two sittings simply because it was so interesting that I could not put it down."

--Dr. Judith Conway Gordon, Retired English Professor and Book Editor

Chapter 1

Quint Cord idly kicked the damp sand at his feet and then wiggled to remove the bits that clung to him. The incoming tide crept closer now licking his toes every seventh wave. Despite an increasing unease, he was too lethargic to move. Closing his eyes, Quint leaned back in the chair willing the images from a few months back to stop invading his mind at every quiet moment. In his role with the CIA he had killed out of necessity in order to keep from being killed or to save others, but never had he been an executioner. The late Representative Douglas Forsyth had deserved everything he got and more, yet it still gnawed at Quint's soul. He did not know why the case haunted him. Even so, he had been in a brooding, self-imposed exile at his home on Figure Eight Island since that fateful event. His friend Gerald Williams, the new Director of the CIA, was beyond annoyed at his continued refusal to accept another assignment. Lila Carson, his on-again, off-again girlfriend, refused to take his calls. Cursing, he stood up and grabbed his chair. He had intended to haul it back a few feet and resume his silent concentration on the far horizon, but a shout from the deck of his house reminded him he was now her personal crusade. The thought caused a wry grin to flicker across his face, the first grin of any kind in months.

Looking up he saw his new housekeeper, Teresa Jones,

waving at him. He glanced down at his watch and saw that it was almost seven. The lowering sun had failed to register on his consciousness. It was time for dinner, and he was in for a scolding as his lunch remained on the table uneaten. He supposed he must be hungry, but if his body was trying to tell him so, it had been awfully quiet about it.

He waved his hand in acknowledgement before bending over to fold up his chair. Slinging it over his shoulder he slogged through the soft sand beyond the tidal reach to the bleached teak walkway that led to his deck. His dog, Code, followed at his heels. The animal was more like a good friend than his dog.

Despite her attempts to reform his bachelor ways, he was glad he had hired Teresa Jones who had previously kept house for the late and unlamented Congressman Forsyth. It was she who had provided the final documentation to bring the man down. Still, he could not help wishing the woman had someone besides him to mother. He leaned the chair against the post at the bottom of the steps and climbed up to the first floor. Like many on the coast, his house was raised on deep-sunk piers that lifted the upper floors above flood range from hurricanes. The ground level, with breakaway walls designed to give against the force of waves to reduce resistance, contained a garage, workshop and storage areas. It also contained a well concealed emergency escape hatch from a safe room on the floor above. Quint climbed the steps to the wide veranda that faced the ocean. The slight chill of the wind at his back warned that fall had arrived.

Waiting just inside the door, Teresa wiped her hands on the ever-present white apron and waved him into the dining room. Quint shook his head, "Why be so formal? You know it would be easier to just let me take dinner in the kitchen with you."

"It wouldn't be proper; no, sir. Not proper at all. That kitchen is for Code and me and I don't need no man messin' around in it. Now you just set on down and eat that dinner. I done and spent hours cookin' it and I shore don't need you to set there and not eat it. You ought to be about starved anyway from not eatin' anything all day. I've always been mighty proud of my cookin' and it don't set right with me you not appreciatin' it. No, sir."

"Not appreciate it?" Quint exclaimed in mock horror. "Haven't I told you what a fabulous chef you are and how lucky I am you agreed to move down here and keep house for me?"

Teresa's smile was smug, "That's right. I do believe you did. Now prove it and eat that dinner."

Quint looked down and nodded his head, "Yes, ma'am."

She stuck her hand in her pocket retrieving a remote, "Here, take this so's you can turn on that music you're so partial to. Now me, I like something a little more soulful than all that classical stuff you play."

Quint sat in his chair and picked up his napkin after first clicking on Marcello's Concert for Oboe in D minor. He didn't know why, but it spoke to the hidden corners of his heart filling him with peace...and yet a yearning. A nice bottle of Chianti was already aerating in the decanter. Realizing that he was ravenous, he appreciatively sniffed his dinner of veal saltimbocca. The wild rice and fresh arugula salad were his favorite side dishes. If he knew Teresa, the meal would end with a perfect tiramisu and espresso. He did not know where the woman had learned to cook the way she had, but she was a genius in the kitchen, rivaling any chef he knew. Once again, he reminded himself how lucky he was to have her.

With a fabulous home on a private island, wealth, youth, a

fabulous cook, a loyal dog, and a sexy, gorgeous girlfriend, he knew he had no reason to continue moping. Watching the waves rolling to shore as the sun slowly sank, he decided it was time to call Lila and try to make amends. To sweeten things up a little so she would take his call, he was going to order a big bouquet of flowers before bedtime.

Just as he finished his dinner, his cell phone rang and without glancing at the caller ID, he answered, "Yes?"

Her voice quavering, Lila said, "I know I've been a little mean, but please, I'm scared. I think I'm in over my head on this latest assignment from Gerald. He's got me tracking some really nasty guys all over the internet and I think they have picked up on me despite all of the roadblocks I've thrown up. They're good, maybe too good."

"Slow down, babe. I'm not mad at you. I can't blame anyone for avoiding me with the funk I've been in. In fact, I was planning to call you later." Quint paused, "So, tell me why you're afraid?"

"I was tracking a terrorist cell a few minutes ago when a screen popped up. It says they know who I am and are coming for me."

"Let's say they have backtracked to your IP address through all of the foils you set up. Does that necessarily mean they can find your exact physical location?"

"It's possible. The other possibility is that this screen is designed to automatically pop up to scare off casual hackers. I've tracked them as far as Brazil. That is not the origin I am almost certain. I suspect from the pattern this guy is leaving that it is somewhere in the Orient; China would be my first guess but I can't exclude Indonesia, India, or somewhere else over there. I would like to think that they can't find me as I have been careful, but I believe these are seriously evil people that are capable of doing some really nasty things. I shudder to even think about it."

"Pack your bag and come on down to Figure Eight. I'll light a fire in the fireplace and have a bottle of champagne waiting. It's time we had a little reunion." Quint could already picture the evening ahead. He grinned in appreciation of the mental images he was busy painting.

"Thank you, I'd love to. Right now, that sounds like heaven. Hopefully you can help me figure out what to do. I should be there by a little after ten." He could hear the smile in her voice. "Hey, I'm sorry I wasn't more understanding of what you go through with this job of yours."

"It's okay. I'm just glad you didn't give up on me. Be careful and make sure you aren't being followed. It wouldn't be a bad idea to drive around no place in particular for a few minutes to see if you pick up a tail."

"And if I do?" Her voice ended on a high note telling him she was genuinely worried.

"Drive to the nearest police station as fast as you can and call me. Hopefully that won't be the case. Let me know when you cross I-95 so I will know when to expect you."

"Will do. See you soon."

Quint walked into the kitchen carrying his plate. The grin that had suffused his face after Lila's call was still on it. Suddenly, he felt whole and happy again. He seriously considered proposing to Lila while she was staying with him. Although he had fought the emotions when he considered his line of work a danger to others that might become attached to him, with Lila also contracting with the CIA it no longer seemed as important. With built-in safety devices in both his home on Figure Eight and the one in Raleigh and with his ability to shoot and fight, he could better protect her with him than when they were apart. On top of that, he wanted to wake up beside her every morning for the rest of their lives. He wanted her to mother his children and give him the warm and loving home he had always craved. With his father a stern and remote figure and his mother dominated by the man, Quinton Cord had grown up lonely. He could manage loneliness. He had for a long time, but he was tired of it.

"Why come you grinnin'?" Teresa planted her arms akimbo and waited. When he sat his dishes on the counter without answering she commented, "Well, somethin' sure done perked you up."

He leaned over and scratched Code behind the ears. "Alright, alright. I have company on the way. Someone special."

"Guess I need to clear up the kitchen and get the guest room freshened up then."

Cord felt himself blush, "No. She'll be staying with me."

Teresa's eyebrows rose so high he thought they would pop off of her head. "Is that right? What ain't you been a tellin' me, boy?"

"As if it is any of your business, Miss Nosy, but Lila is my longtime girlfriend and I'm seriously considering making her something more."

"Good. If she can make you smile and look happy like you do now, I already love that girl."

"Do we have any champagne left in the fridge?"

"We do and I can rustle up something for that gal to eat when she gets here. What time you figure it will be?"

"She said she was going to throw some things into a bag and leave right away. It's only a couple of hours drive, so I figure she will be here by 10:30 latest. She's going to call me when she crosses 95, so I figure it will be about an hour and a half from there. I'll let you know."

"Soon as I finish up here, I'll cut some of them flowers in the garden before it gets pitch black. I'm going to change your sheets and towels and neaten up your bedroom. Want me to stick some candles in there, too?"

"Lila's easy, so don't knock yourself out."

"Maybe, but I still intend to make her feel mighty welcome."

"That makes two of us. And yeah, candles would be nice." Quint wagged his eyebrows suggestively.

"You behave your bad self." Teresa was laughing as he wandered back onto the deck and stared out to sea.

Quint sat in a deck chair sipping on a glass of wine and watching the minutes tick by on his clock. The sound of music from the speaker above his head should have been soothing but was not. When nine o'clock arrived and he had still heard nothing, he dialed Lila's phone and got no answer, thus increasing his worry. By nine-thirty he was past worried and pacing the deck, Code dogging his heels as though he was helping him worry. Again, he listened to the ringing of her phone until the automated answering response came on. "Lila, call me as soon as you get this message. I was expecting to hear from you at least an hour ago. Let me know where you are."

Quint hung up the phone not sure what to do next. Walking down the steps to the teak walkway to the beach, he walked to the end where again he stared at the dark moonlit sea and waited. He kept looking at his phone as though the mere act of looking would make it ring. When ten thirty came and he had still heard nothing, he hesitated no longer. Dialing Gerald Williams' number, he waited for the man to answer.

The minute he heard the answering click, he did not wait for Gerald to say anything but hurriedly blurted, "Gerald, something has happened to Lila. She was to be at Figure Eight by now. She was leaving because she's scared. The targets you put her onto threatened to take her out. I have called repeatedly, and she doesn't answer. I know something is wrong. She was to have called me when she crossed Interstate 95, and she didn't do that either."

"Yeah, she told me about the message in an email earlier and said she was on her way to you." Gerald sighed, "Crap. Listen, Quint, try not to worry if you can. I'm going to get my assistant to start calling around to see if he can pick up on anything. I'll get one of our local guys to go by her house and then follow up with the police and hospitals. We'll pick up her computer and try to do a trace on what she has been tracking. As soon as I know anything, I'll let you know. In the meantime, let's hope her phone is off and she's just late arriving. So, if she does get there, let me know."

"No problem, but at this point my gut tells me something is badly wrong or she would be here. I don't like it one damned bit."

Gerald's voice was sad when he replied, "Frankly neither do I. Now, let me get on it. I'll call you as soon as I learn anything."

"Thanks."

Quint slid his cell phone into his pocket and walked back into the house. "Teresa," he called.

"Yes, sir. Your girl here?" She walked into the living room as she answered, looking around expectantly for the anticipated girlfriend.

"No, she's not. I think she's in trouble. Put the food away and go on to bed. If I don't hear from her shortly, I'm driving to Raleigh to see what's happened. I'll call you in the morning if I leave tonight."

"Lordy, I sure am sorry to hear that. I'm a goin' to be prayin' that girl's alright."

Teresa walked up to him and patted his shoulder, "You let me know if you hear anything. I ain't goin' to be sleepin' for worryin;' so if that's the case, let me know before you leave. In the meantime, we will just pray she gets here."

"Thanks, Teresa. I appreciate it." Quint walked back onto the deck and sank down into the cushioned comfort of the deck chair. He picked up his wine glass and resumed staring at the sea, willing the sound of her car in the driveway to break the music of the waves. Code came and sat down beside him with his muzzle against his leg as though to offer comfort. Quint reached down and stroked the dog in gratitude for his love. After twenty minutes he had had enough. "Code, old buddy, I am out of here and leaving you with Teresa. Something is wrong with Lila, dammit, and I intend to find out what it is."

Code stood up and stared at him, growling low in his throat. There were times when he swore the dog knew what he was saying. Now was one of them.

Quint shook his head, "No, not this time. I have no clue what I might run into. You are better off here."

The dog hung his head and followed him to the bedroom. Quint threw his things into an overnighter and gave Code a hug goodbye. He whispered, "I love you, boy. Be good for Teresa."

Teresa was waiting for him at the door. "You be careful now. I don't know what has happened, but with all that CIA stuff you're mixed up in, I do stay a mite worried."

"It isn't me in trouble this time, Teresa. It's Lila. I need to find out what she has gotten into and where she is. Don't worry. I'll keep you posted. Thanks for taking care of my dog for me. Right now he's pouting, but a treat or two should put things right. And, Teresa, remember to set the alarms…and if you need to, get to the safe room."

"I know; I remember. As for Code, he's good company for me. So, don't worry about us. We're going to get along just fine."

Both Teresa and Code were standing on the deck to see him off when he drove from the house. The porch light made her grizzled hair almost look almost white. With one hand she restrained Code so he would not try to follow. In the rear-view mirror, he could see them turn and go inside. The sight gave him a warm glow. For the first time in years he felt as though he truly had a home, one that needed the woman he loved in it. He just had to find her and keep her safe. Quint cursed himself for telling Gerald Williams about her talent with the Web. He should have known the CIA would want her skills. Now her life was at risk thanks to his big mouth. He swore softly and turned on the radio.

He had barely reached Interstate 40 when his phone rang. He glanced at the screen hoping it was Lila calling. It wasn't. He wasted no time. "Gerald, what have you learned?"

Chapter 2

Chen Dai clicked his ballpoint pen as he watched the moving dot on the screen. He had discovered someone tracking him a couple of weeks earlier. For days Dai patiently followed the circuitous route to his tracker. At the discovery he wanted to stand up and shout his triumph for the others in the office to hear. But that would not do. Such emotion was unseemly in China and particularly in the Baiduru Company. One day they would realize his genius, but by then he would have gone on to bigger things, much bigger. He sneered at the red dot. How dare she try to track him? His tracker was persistent, having followed the convoluted pathway from the company's US office near Seattle to Brazil. That was only a step away from finding his actual location. Despite all the roadblocks he had installed to mask his IP address, the tracker was too good for him to risk leaving her out there. It had taken him days to ferret out her identity, address, and the serial number of her car. From that point on, he was in control. That was as it should be: he was the best at these games.

Unbeknownst to his tracker, his current job was ideal for the kind of operations his master plan required and for eliminating any threats that might crop up. The Baiduru Company was a leader in Web management, at the forefront of autonomous navigation technology, and advancing the field of artificial intelligence. Although he knew little credit would come to him, and certainly no more money in his paycheck, it was his work that Baiduru was using as a ladder to achieving even greater advances in the various fields. Eventually, he would not need Baiduru at all. In the meantime, his situation was a fertile field in which to grow his ambitions. Using the Baiduru platform, he developed a worm that he implanted into a Chinese GPS satellite that covered almost all of Asia from Siberia to Indonesia. With a few strokes of the keyboard, he had access to much of the navigation in the region. North Korea, with a paranoid madman at the helm, was a problem but he was working to solve that as well. What his company didn't know about his clandestine work would not hurt him.

He watched the red dot on the computer screen as it left the city. He would do nothing until she was on the open highway and well away from any large hospitals or emergency vehicles before he would strike. The weather report for the target's location showed a line of heavy thunderstorms moving through the area. That would further tie up emergency responses. He continued clicking his pen as the dot moved further from Raleigh. It would not be long now.

He looked up in irritation as the intercom on the wall squawked. He was being paged to go to his immediate director's office to help with some problem or other. Why couldn't the stupid fool find someone else to repair his screw-ups? Dai ignored the summons and resumed clicking his pen. Perhaps another forty minutes or so and then this particular problem would vanish.

A head popped up from the neighboring cubicle. His friend, Zhao Wen, hissed, "Dai, do you not hear the page? The director is in hot water I am told. You are going to have to go save his ass again, and this time it's going to take some doing. I suspect he's going to have your nose to the grindstone for the rest of the day and into the night."

"I'm tied up with something I can't leave. Let the jerk wait a few minutes. It won't kill him," Dai growled in response.

Wen whispered, "Keep your voice down. That attitude can get you fired if the jerk finds out."

Dai knew he had no choice. He had to answer the page or consequences would be dire. It wasn't ideal but with his target twenty miles out of the city, it would have to do. That decided, he looked back at his keyboard and punched in the proper codes. A slow smile crossed his face when the red dot on the monitor stopped moving.

There was no time to gloat as the page again came for him to report. Logging out he hastened to the director's office. When he entered the office, he was greeted by his superior's harsh glare. Huang Changpu was a tyrant who had little knowledge of the division he led, having weaseled his way in due to his high rank in the local communist party. He covered his ignorance with bluster and heavy-handed authority. Dai had no respect for the posturing idiot, but he was too smart to let his contempt show. Huang was just one small obstacle among many on the way to achieving his goal.

While Director Huang explained the problem, Dai was expected to repair, Dai only half listened once he realized how simple the fix would be, allowing his attention to wander. In his mind, he was planning his next steps. He did not at first hear Huang's dismissal.

Huang barked, "I said take care of this and leave my office, Chen. I have more important things to do than to sit here staring at you."

"My apologies, Director Huang," Dai said as he first bowed and then backed from the office. Once he had closed the door, he straightened and muttered 'screw you, you piece of dog shit.'

He wasted no time bringing his computer back on-line. First, he repaired the director's tangle of errors. Next, he typed in the address of his contact in North Korea. Finding Pah Pong Ju was pure luck. He had run into the man in a bar in Wanson, a new resort on the east coast of North Korea, designed to cater to foreigners. Over beer, the two men had commiserated with one another in low voices while the noise of the bar drowned their conversation to any eves-droppers. Chen Dai figured he had just solved much of his access problem into the North Korean satellite system. Soon it would have his virus, fondly named Dragnav, firmly implanted.

Pah Pong Ju was an angry man. Shortly after Kim Jong-Un became President of the People's Republic of North Korea, Pah's father was murdered. General Pah had sided with Kim Jong-Un's uncle, Jang Song-thaek. Arrested for plotting a coup to overthrow the Kim regime and replace it with one friendlier to China, Jang was taken to a show trial and executed. His death was followed by the execution of over 300 supposed co-conspirators.

A general in the army, Pah's father had become a major target of the purge. After his trial and death, Pong Ju's mother had committed suicide at the loss of status and financial means. His father had called to warn him well before the arrest to disappear from the university for a few months. Pah had quietly slipped away that night and was working in the port of Wanson when Dai met him. H never returned to his studies. An only child of dead parents, both directly and indirectly at Kim Jong-Un's hand, he hated the president with ferocity. Publicly disowning his father, he patiently worked his way into a tech job with a Korean shipping company. He walked a careful line to appear outwardly docile and supportive of Kim. Any slip and the middle-aged woman in his apartment complex, the official Inminban, would report him to the police. Pah Pong Ju lived in fear of the Kyuch'aldae, the mobile police unit that could burst into one's home at any moment to look for subversive materials. Whispered stories about Kwanliso, the prison for political dissidents, were sufficient to make him very wary.

For a time following his parents' deaths he considered defecting to Chosun, the North Korean name for South Korea. However frequent demands to appear before the Bowibu, the National Security Agency responsible for investigating political crimes, assured him that because of his father he was being closely watched. It would take careful planning and years of plotting and saving money before that became a possibility. In the meantime, he was much more fortunate than most with access to enough food to avoid starvation, the fate of far too many of his countrymen.

Due to Pah Pong Ju's family's traditional status or song-bien in the strict caste system and a high-ranking uncle, he still enjoyed privileges denied most of his countrymen. Had it not been for that, his exceptional intelligence, and computational skills, his father's death would have reduced him to the lowest caste. When Kim's power and prestige were diminished, he would work with those friends of his father and Kim's uncle who had managed to survive the purge, to rebuild his country.

Pah's hatred would be the sword Dai used to achieve both men's goals. Pong Ju supplied the information Dai needed to begin attacks on computer-operated systems in shipping, the military, and factories in North Korea through the GPS satellite system. Between them, Pah and Chen devised an email address which Dragnav would recognize as friendly thereby allowing access to the top-secret, encrypted database controlling access to software algorithms on the North Korean satellite. Once back in China, Chen disguised the Dragnav worm to avoid North Korean military antivirus detection. He was proud of his creation, one that dynamically changed location on the satellite's computer every 46 minutes. It also changed the number of bytes it occupied at the same interval. With both the Chinese and North Korean GPS systems compromised, all he needed to do to gain control was to send new coordinates to any targeted vessel in the satellite coverage area. The next step was to embed the worm into the US satellite over the China Sea. Once he had Dragnav implanted in all three, he would control all navigation in the region. That was only the beginning. From the first three, he would expand to implant Dragnav in satellite GPS systems across the globe. Chen smiled. He would soon control the world. Every country would be at his feet begging.

Pah's job within the conglomerate company of Myohyang Shipping in Phyongyang allowed him access to the infrastructure that he would destroy in order to take Kim Jong-Un down. Together they would purge Pong Ju's homeland of the vicious, cult-like, demi-god ruler. Pong Ju was not even curious as to why Dai would help him. The man's colossal ego no doubt played a role, but Pah did not care what Dai might hope to achieve beyond ego gratification, as long as he helped him achieve his own goals.

When he heard his computer ping announcing a text message, he quickly shut the door to his office and turned the lock. Using the friendly log-on that he and Dai had devised, he scanned the long-awaited message. He was ready with the information needed to begin his campaign to bring down Kim.

When Pong Ju logged off with Dai he was an unhappy man, unhappy and frustrated. While he wanted to target only military transportation of various types, Dai was unready to go there until he had perfected the ability to penetrate the North Korean cyber defenses in such a way as to preclude trace-ability to him. Until he was sure that he could proceed to the next level, he insisted they begin with a smaller target that was not as likely to receive the same scrutiny. Pah could understand the caution; however, the last thing he wanted was to instigate the loss of civilian lives. He had listened to Dai's reasoning that such loss would also bring condemnation against a government that did not exert sufficient safety regulations over non-military transportation. In theory he could accept that; however, the loss of innocent lives was troubling to him, especially since he was the one that would be the root cause. In the end, he agreed to send the necessary information for Dai's first target. He agreed because as Dai pointed out, Dai did not need him as much as he needed Dai. While he had access to critical information, he did not have the autonomy to act, nor the computer skills that made Dai so valuable to him. The Chinaman had not hesitated to point that out to Pah Pong Ju. The threat was clear. Unless he played it Dai's way, he would have to abandon his plan to destroy Kim Jong Un.

Pah spent the next hour researching vessels that would be carrying the fewest number of passengers. He might not have any say in the type of vessel targeted but he could pick the ones that would cause the fewest deaths. That should be enough to see if the authorities would bother to check the reason behind the disaster or just ignore it beyond an official statement of sympathy for the victims.

After careful research, Pah settled on the ferry run between the ports of Namp'o and Songrim on the Taedong River west of Phongyang as the one least likely to have a large number of civilians. Satisfied he had done the best he could to mitigate the deaths of innocent people; he sent the vessel statistics, registration number, and schedule to Dai. Soon he would know what he had caused. With few private automobiles and poorly maintained and limited roadways, river vessels were often the best mode of transport for those with government permission to travel. Small boats on the inland waterways had no sophisticated computerized navigational system. The only ones he could target through a computer were military and commercial…the ones least likely to haul a large number of civilians.

Pah Pong Ju glanced at the clock, it was time to leave for the day. He shut down his computer, grabbed his coat and left the office to walk to the nearest cafe with a television. Normally, he didn't bother with television, as it was an endless stream of state propaganda; however, tonight he wanted to be there when the ferry went down in the Taedong River. He wanted to see whether or not Dai had the ability to do what he promised or if he was just so much arrogant boasting. If all went as planned, he would have only a couple of hours wait.

Miles away in China, Chen Dai was late leaving for the evening, giving as the excuse the need to correct the problem his director had assigned him. Using the information Pah had provided, Dai had logged into the Korean ferry's GPS system in less than ten minutes. It took mere moments to open his satellite implanted virus and find another vessel on the same route but traveling in the opposite direction. He didn't need to break into that vessel's navigational system. All he needed were coordinates for plotting the time of closest distance to the targeted ferry. Soon the dots indicating the two ships were glowing on his screen as they steadily approached one another. Typing in the command to veer right just before the two ships were slated to pass in opposite directions, Dai watched as the ferry moved into the path of the heavily loaded on-coming freighter too late to avoid a collision. He smiled with satisfaction.

Pah was not smiling. He had just finished the last of his beer when the program he was watching was interrupted by a message of a ferry disaster on the Taedong River killing 47 children who were on a state sponsored fieldtrip. Pah tried to tell himself that he had no way of knowing the passenger list of the ferry, and therefore, was not responsible for their deaths; but deep inside he knew he was damned as the worst kind of murderer. He may not have operated the computer that changed the ferry's route, but he had provided the necessary information to do so.

Pah watched the flickering screen in silent remorse. Suddenly the man he hated more than any other filled the screen. The dictator screamed abuse at the captain of the ship vowing to punish the captain and his family causing them as much pain as the man had caused so many families now wailing in agony at the loss of their beloved children. Pah snorted in derision. He knew the man cared nothing for his people's woes. He only wanted to circumvent any blame coming back to his regime. He shook his head sadly at the price the innocent captain and his family would pay. He could only hope that they managed to escape before Kim Jung-Un's henchmen came for them. He laid the price of his drink on the counter and turned his back on the television that had switched to scenes of screaming, angry parents demanding retribution for their children's deaths.

As he edged past other diners to the door of the cafe, he reminded himself that he was in a silent war against a brutal regime that would not hesitate to take innocent lives, that all wars invariably affected the innocent in one way or another. However, he knew that his mother and father, already restless spirits due to the nature of their deaths, would be even more restless after the sins he had committed against his family's honor. No matter his father's involvement in the plot to bring down the dictator's regime, the general would never have stained the honor of his family by committing such an atrocity as the one for which his son was now responsible.

Pah, like many Koreans both north and south, had maintained a belief in shamanism through centuries of layered spiritual beliefs composed of various religious ideologies. In the modern Koreas, such superstition was seen as shameful and belonging to the ignorant peasant class to which his own family had never belonged. With education and privilege, land ownership and ruling status through the centuries, they represented the peak of society and yet still clung to old beliefs never publicly admitted by the ruling class, and now by none.

Pah left the restaurant and walked the long way to his lonely apartment. He was so lost in thought the kochebi…abandoned or orphaned homeless starving children…that followed him failed to illicit the usual twinge of guilt. Without breaking stride he dropped a few coins on the street where they were quickly snatched. The vision of screaming children as they drowned in the foul waters of the river tormented him. He had to find some answer, some peace. He could not go on otherwise. Despite his desire to bring down the Kim Jong-Un regime, he had never intended to become a murderer of innocent children. He refused to consider that the pilots of military planes and ships might in their own way be as innocent as the children. Somehow, when he thought of the military under the thrall of the Kim regime, he did not see them as worthy of any guilt, were they to die at his hand. When he reached his door, his mind was made up. He would go to the shaman that would guide him to his father's spirit, and he would ask for direction and absolution.

Although not a follower of Sinism, he was superstitious, and the murders of innocent children weighed heavily on his conscience. Haneullim, the supreme being, would not allow his soul into a peaceful hereafter until he made peace with his father and his ancestors. Pah was convinced his father, despite being a military man, would have drawn a line at the actions instigated by his son. When he reached his door, he unlocked it and walked into the kitchen where his cook had left a bap or meal of Shabu-shabu warming in the small oven and poured himself a drink. Although he rarely took alcohol, tonight he needed it to still the shaking in his hands. Taking a seat at the wooden table that was crammed into the corner, he seasoned the thinly sliced beef noodles with a sesame sauce before taking a small sip of the ubiquitous rough corn liquor that he kept on hand. Once the shaking stopped, he picked up his cell phone. Scrolling through his contacts he found the name he sought. Although most mudangs were female, he remembered the male shaman or baksu mudang that his father had occasionally visited. The shaman's phone rang repeatedly, and Pah was ready to hang up when the baksu mudang at last answered.

Pah hurried to explain his call, "I am Pah Pong Ju the son of

General Pah who visited you from time to time."

Jadu Hyun's voice was soft when he replied, "I remember the General. Are you in need of communing with his spirit, my son?"

"I would like to visit you for the Gut ceremony and the purification ritual as I fear something, I have done makes the spirit of my father restless."

An hour later, Pah sat on the cushion in Jadu's front room while the costumed man-made offerings to the gods, sang and danced rhythmically and offered prayers...all in the sacred groups of three. When that was done, he sat across from Pah and grew silent while he waited for the spirit of General Pah to appear to him so he could intercede on behalf of his son.

Pah Jong Ju felt perspiration bead his forehead while he waited for the spirit of his father to speak to the baksu mudang. He could understand nothing of the shaman's mutterings but because of the intensity of the man's expression he felt that he was beginning to break through to the spirit realm. A sudden sharp intake of the shaman's breath followed by even more agitated murmurings, increased Pah's alarm. Cold chills shook him as he felt the force of his father's spirit around him. Swallowing hard to keep a sudden sob from escaping, he forced himself to remain still when all he wanted to do was flee into the concealing darkness of the night. After a time, the mudang grew quiet.

Pah waited with bated breath for Jadu's words.

The shaman, small and hunched by age, looked into his eyes. "Your father is restless and alarmed for his son. He fears that you have brought shame to your ancestors. He asks that you remember his fate and that of your mother and realize the danger of your path. I was your father's friend as well as his spirit guide, so I tell you as a friend that these are dangerous times for men of virtue. And you, my son, despite your actions, that I can only sense, are virtuous in your heart."

Pah hung his head in shame. He wanted to confess but the mudang's wrinkled, aged-spotted hand reached out stilling the words on Pah's tongue. "No, Pah Pong Ju. I do not need to hear what disturbed your soul and your father's spirit. It is not safe. Now we must perform the bakjan and drink a cup of wine for purification. Then we will burn white paper to further purify and bring peace to your spirit and propitiation to your ancestors."

Chapter 3

Quint opened the door into the IC unit and walked to the small room where Lila lay surrounded by blinking monitors. She looked so small and defenseless in the hospital bed with her bandage-swathed head and battered and bruised arms that lay outside the blankets and connected to a myriad of tubes. He pulled a chair close to the bedside. Although he had been warned that she had not yet regained consciousness, he could not help taking her hand and talking to her as though she could hear.

"I need you to wake up, Lila. Talk to me and tell me what happened." Quint steadied his voice and continued, "I am so sorry I ever talked you into letting Gerald Williams call you and offer you a job with the Agency. I knew it was dangerous, too dangerous for someone I care about. I wish you would wake up so I could tell you how much you matter to me. I have wanted so long to tell you, please..."

Quint stopped. Tears clogged his throat and slowly rolled down his cheeks. His head was bent against her hand on the bed as he held it. He did not hear the door open or someone enter. He felt a hand on his shoulder rubbing as though to give comfort but did not look up. It barely registered through his despair. He became aware that someone was talking to him. Lifting his head and surreptitiously wiping his eyes to clear them, he sat up in his chair and turned. Looking up, his eyes met those of the CIA director, his friend Gerald Williams.

"No change?" Gerald inquired.

Quint shook his head, still unable to talk.

"I'm sorry, Quint. It hurts to see someone you care about like this. I know how I would feel if it were Jill or one of my boys."

Quint nodded his head, "Yeah, it's tough. I just want to find whoever did this to her and make them pay. She was on to someone, some hacker that warned her to back off. God only knows, she is the last one to let go once she sinks her teeth in. I can't help but feel that is what caused her accident."

"I wouldn't be surprised. My guys are going over her car with a fine-toothed comb to see if something malfunctioned, if the brake lines were cut, or what else may have happened. It's possible someone tried to run her off the road, but we have no other vehicle implicated in this judging by an initial examination of her car. We also cannot rule out that she was nervous and in a hurry and maybe lost control in the curve."

"No way. Yeah, she was scared, but she was too careful to do that. Nope, I am convinced this is an attempt to stop her from getting any closer to the hacker."

"I'm inclined to agree. Our guys are the best at what they do. When they find something…and they will one way or another… I'll let you know." Gerald paused, "When you are ready, we need you to come back to work. While she is in a coma, you can do more to help her by finding who is responsible than you can by just worrying."

Quint eyes were as cold as blue steel when he looked up. "I'm not leaving this bed until she is out of danger. Once she's in the clear, you are damned straight I'll find who did this, whether I'm with the Agency or not."

"I don't have to tell you that job will be a lot easier with our resources than it will with you out there on your own."

Refusing a commitment, Quint shrugged his shoulders. "The doctor hasn't yet made his rounds. I'm hoping he can tell me something about her condition."

"I'll stick around a little longer. I would like to hear that myself. Then I'm going to have to get back to Washington. The President wants me at a meeting about some strange shipping accidents in the Far East. A couple of them were vessels in our navy; the other was North Korean. Both our guys and the Korean captain swear it was like they lost all navigational control of their ships. From the intelligence so far, the President seems to think their computer steering system was compromised. It could be Korean's just trying to cover ass as a bunch of kids died in the accident and folks are baying for his hide. As for ours, I don't have a clue at this point."

"That captain may have a point. It seems to me we pulled that stunt ourselves when we took out that crook, Congressman Forsyth." Quint snorted, "I wish all of the North Korean ships would have an accident and the planes, too."

Gerald did not want to get into a discussion of the Congressman's death and chose to ignore that part of Quint's remarks. "Don't we all? I would more like to see the missile launchers taken out along with silos and manufacturing plants for warheads. The madman running the show is a problem that should have been stamped out long ago. It pisses me off that this whole mess could have been resolved. Now, here we are with nuclear warheads looming on our own horizon. Too many pansy-asses didn't have the nerve then, and they still don't."

"Hey, you run the spook show. What's stopping you from taking the son of a bitch out?"

It was Gerald's turn to snort, "I may run it, but I don't call all the shots. There are a hell of a lot of hoops to jump through between here and there."

"We can always run around those hoops. We have before."

"Yeah, but they didn't have the same threat that the situation poses with the North Koreans, South Koreans, Chinese, Russians, Japanese, and Iranians all in the mix. It's a real can of worms."

Both men stopped talking. Gerald sat in the other chair in the room and alternated his focus from the silent clock to the ticking of the monitor beside Lila's bed. He noticed that Quint was doing much the same.

An hour later doctor rounds interrupted their quiet contemplation. Dr. Allen Smithson, the Irish-complexioned neurological specialist, had been both blunt and sympathetic to Quint's inquiries.

When he left, Gerald rose and ran his hands through his hair. Quint could not help noticing that he was rapidly going grayer. "You're leaving?"

"Yeah, I can do more good trying to find out what happened than sitting here. I know you will keep me informed if there's any change. Just remember the positive things the doctor said. She's young and in good health. And you and I know she is a fighter. If anyone can pull through this, she can."

"I know..." Quint looked down and then up into Gerald's eyes, "I want her to make it, but if she has to live her life like some mindless vegetable, she would not want to live. I understand that's just one possibility among others with this kind of brain injury. I just want her back like she was."

"We all do." Changing tactics, Gerald asked, "Is there anyone else we need to notify about her accident?"

"I'm sure you saw in the background check that she was an only child and her parents are both dead. To the best of my knowledge she didn't have any close relatives as the family had about petered out. As for friends or cohorts from her former job at the university, I really can't say since she never really talked about them."

Gerald nodded his head, "Hang in there. As soon as I hear something from the forensics on her car, I'll let you know. Call me if Lila comes out of the coma and is able to talk about what happened."

"Absolutely. And thanks. I appreciate you coming. I know Lila would have, too."

Gerald reached out and patted Quint's shoulder, "Later. And think positive. Right now, that is the best message you can communicate to her."

It was less than four hours later that Gerald received the report on Lila's car. It revealed a sum total of nothing...no tampering, no apparent malfunction, no reason for the crash except driver error. He sat at his desk tapping his pencil, but put it down before he broke yet another. It was an old habit and it helped him think. While the report found no physical link to some nefarious outside agency or agent, with electronic interference something beyond Lila could have caused the accident. Until she regained consciousness, there would be no answers. If she could not remember, there still would be none. He called Quint who was firmly ensconced at the hospital bedside and told him the results of the inspection. Quint refused to accept that it was somehow driver error. He was convinced that the accident was the result of someone trying to stop Lila's tracking. While he did not voice it, Gerald agreed.

Dr. Smithson encouraged Quint to spend as much time with Lila as possible. Without family to help, Quint felt that he had to stay. While science could not prove that a comatose patient could hear and process what was being said, the doctor suspected that something might get through and thus Quint talked.

A week later, Quint was hoarse from talking. He was bored with the monotonous repetition of everything that he had chattered about during the days of bedside vigil. He was frustrated that Lila continued to be unresponsive to any stimuli. He sensed the doctor's concern that there was no indication of her coming out of the coma. He was sick of hospital food. He ached from trying to sleep in the narrow reclining chair by the window of her room. His clothes were stale and he was too. All in all, he felt pretty low. Even, Gerald's daily calls did not help...especially since the director knew no more than he had a week ago. Quint could not help but think that there must be something he could do besides talk and stew. The blinking light on his computer, fully charged and still plugged in, taunted him. Unfortunately, he lacked Lila's skills in cyberspace and rued that even were he to try, he would have wasted time. Better to keep talking and praying he decided.

He did not know how long he dosed but something had awakened him. He looked at his watch. It was three in the morning. The low hum of the various monitoring machines, the distant noises of a never sleeping hospital ward, and the low lights were all the same as when he had reclined in the narrow chair, stuffed a pillow under his head, and pulled up the ubiquitous white hospital blanket. For a moment he lay still, confused as to why he had awakened. Hearing nothing out of the ordinary, he fluffed his pillow and turned on his side. He had not yet drifted into sleep, when a low moan from the bed aroused him to full alertness. Tossing back the blanket and returning the chair to upright, he slipped on his shoes and walked over to the bed. Lila was moving and moaning softly.

"Wake up, babe. I need you to come back to me. Come on now. Open your eyes. Talk to me, darling. Come on, Lila. You are a fighter. You can do it. You can."

Quint picked up her hand and gave it a squeeze, "Come on, babe. Wake up."

At first, he thought he had imagined the flutter of her eyelids before they closed. After several anxious minutes while he encouraged her to wake up, Lila opened her eyes briefly before again closing them.

"That's right, babe. Come on, now!" Quint used his free hand to grab the call button to summon a nurse. While he awaited her arrival, he continued to urge Lila to talk to him. Quint felt as excited as he had as a kid when he raced down the steps to see what Santa Claus had left during the night.

The night nurse ambled into the room with no apparent rush or interest. Quint took an immediate dislike to her calm and somewhat bored expression and his hackles went up. "Sweet Jesus, you folks sure do take your time getting here."

She smiled. Her voice was dripping with barely concealed tolerance for yet another overwrought family member. "What seems to be the problem?"

"I don't know that there is a problem. I signaled you to come because I think Lila is coming out of the coma and you should know."

Nurse Rachitt, he immediately named her in his mind, walked over to Lila and studied both her and the monitor. "I don't see any change. I'm certain you want her to come out of this. However, you realize that may not happen. The doctor warned you. It's the middle of the night. You have had little rest. Perhaps, you dreamed it."

"Do not condescend to me. I am fully aware of the hour and my lack of any real rest in that damned chair you call a bed. However, I am not delusional, and I swear she opened her eyes. The doctor asked me to immediately notify the staff if there were any changes. You can consider yourself notified."

"Yes, thank you." She nodded at the woman in the bed, "Now, if she opens her eyes and they stay open, then she's making progress. Until then, I suggest you try to get some rest. It isn't necessary to stay. As you are aware, this is a step-down ICU unit with only three patients per nurse. If there is any real change, we can call you. Why don't you go home and try to sleep?"

Tamping down his annoyance, Quint replied, "Why don't you go back to your little desk and don't worry about me. I will be here the next time she opens her eyes."

"That's your choice of course." The nurse checked the IV bags, took temperature and pulse and entered the readings on the computer anchored to the wall across from the bed. That done, she exited the room...leaving Quint to glare at her retreating backside.

He continued to babble to Lila after the nurse left. He no longer knew what he was saying. He just talked. His words came further and further apart and soon he was nodding in the chair.

Dawn came with creeping fingers of light crossing the floor, and as the sun rose higher, shone on Quint's closed eyes. Sitting up, he blinked himself into awareness and stretched to relieve aching muscles. He studied Lila for a moment, and detecting no change, he walked into the bathroom to relieve an overly full bladder. He flushed the toilet and went to the sink to wash his hands. Catching a glimpse of his face in the mirror, he opened his eyes in surprise. With the beginnings of a beard he had not taken time to shave, and days of fatigue and worry, he suddenly looked far older than his 33 years. He shook his head at the reflected image.

After procuring a razor and shaving soap from the nurse' station he proceeded to remove the days of stubble from his face. He stepped into the shower and let jets of hot water beat onto his head and muscles bringing relief to various pains. He then toweled himself dry and looked with disgust at the things he had been wearing. His clothes were wrinkled and smelled from too many days of wear and the toxic odor of adrenalin driven perspiration. At some point he would need to leave Rex Hospital and drive the few miles to his Raleigh house on Park Dr. to change clothes. The things he had worn were past redemption. However, at the moment he had no choice but to put them back on. He waved them in the air for a minute. Lifting them to his nose he inhaled the still rank odor. Disgusted at the need, he put them on, zipped his pants and buttoned his shirt, slipped on his shoes but stuffed his socks into the trash receptacle. He didn't care to ever see them again. That done he returned to Lila's bedside and resumed his vigil.

At 7:30 a brief rap on the doorjamb alerted him to Dr. Smithson's arrival. "Good morning, Quint. The nurse tells me you think Lila is beginning to come around. Have you had any further indication since last night?"

"No. I fell asleep not long after the nurse was in and when I woke up, I took a shower. I've only been awake maybe 15 minutes."

"Why don't you see if you can rouse her?"

Quint picked up Lila's hand and rubbed it, "Can you wake up for me, sweetheart? I so much want to see your beautiful eyes looking into mine. I want to talk to you and I want you to talk to me. I want to tell you how much I love you and need you in my life. Come on, Lila. Open your eyes, or at least, squeeze my hand."

Both he and the doctor waited with bated breath only to find no response from the comatose woman. Dr. Smithson's gaze was full of pity when he said, "Quint, are you sure you did not dream her eyes opening?

Chapter 4

Chen Dai leaned back on the sofa with a self-satisfied smile on his face. He sipped the cocktail he had just mixed and savored the astringent flavor. A slow smile of self-satisfaction lit up his saturnine features. Soon the world would recognize his genius. Soon the world would appreciate his power. Very soon, they would all turn to him for the salvation only he could provide. Then...then he would be in command of them all. No one would ever have been as powerful as he with the right to life or death over anyone he chose, anywhere he chose. Nations would quake before him. People would speak his name with awe and terror. The North Korean, Pah Pong Ju, was a bit of a problem. The man's sensitivities to his ancestors was concerning. Perhaps it was time for a serious discussion with Mr. Pah.

Chen Dai leaned forward and set his cocktail on the table. Logging on to his computer he dialed Pah Pong Ju and waited for the answer. He had almost tapped the key to log out when Pong Ju answered. Dai wasted no time in launching his attack.

"This is no game here. We are both in too deep to back out now. You have the information to bring me down...possibly. However, my tracks are carefully covered and it will be difficult to prove I had anything to do with the ferry incident. You, unfortunately, are very vulnerable."

"Is this a threat?"

"I am not threatening at all. I am merely pointing out some

truths that we should both be cognizant of. I have no desire to reveal my source of information in North Korea. You are much too valuable for that. And you cannot reveal me without disclosing your own part in the ferry sinking. The question is can I trust you to continue in a confidential and supportive manner in what we have already determined is a mutual course of action?"

"I am willing to attack the military component of Kim Jong Un's regime, but I am not going to provide you with anything more that could harm innocent people."

"That's fine, Pong Ju. You need to relax. We neither one knew that children would be on the ferry. Surely you do not think me that monstrous?"

"Look, I don't know the reason you are doing what you're doing. I don't suppose I really care. All I want to do is avenge the murder of my father and the needless death of my mother and bring down the fat little dictator that is strangling my country. That is all I want. I will help you do that if I can, but not without your assurance that we will not kill innocent women and children. Kim's military and his minions I am happy to lead you to."

"But, of course. I have already acknowledged the regrettable loss of those children on board the ferry. Now, let's move forward. It isn't unexpected to have a few mistakes early on. We must simply assure we have no more of that nature."

"I agree."

"Shall we move on then and see what our next target should be. Have you been thinking of something that might sting the mighty Kim Jong Un?"

"I have. But first I have to ascertain whether or not I can assess the information you need."

"How long do you think that will take?"

"A week or two at most."

"That shouldn't be a problem. I want to tweak a few vulnerable giants while you get your information."

"Who are they?"

"Come now, Pong Ju. You know you don't really want to know."

"I suppose not." Pong Ju listened to the soft click that informed him Chen Dai was no longer on the other end.

Chen Dai smiled to himself as he settled against the cushions and took another sip of his drink. He loved the name his parents had given him. Combined with his surname it meant sword of the dragon. He intended to live up to his name and make war with the sword of technology.

The screen glowed with blinking dots. Some of them he could identify, others he would in future. For now, there were enough targets available for his next step. Typing in instructions, he settled back into his chair, sipped his drink and randomly selected his target. At this point it did not really matter to him. What mattered was the test of his ability to access any of the targets in his range of control. He grinned with all of the glee of a teenager playing war games on a computer as he watched the blinking dot converge on the selected target. The United States would not like the repercussions of this one. The dot represented a plane that he now controlled. He grinned as he watched it draw ever closer to the target. With the flaperon actuators out of commission and the throttle on full forward, they were moments from collision with a Chinese aircraft. In his mind he pictured the frantic crew as they tried to avoid a collision that might easily destroy any peace between the two great powers as well as cost their own lives.

The US Marine Corps Air Station at Futenma on the Island of Okinawa, Japan, currently flew over two dozen MV-22 Ospreys. Dai laughed as the plane neared the selected target from PLAAF. The People's Liberation Army Air Force, now the largest in Asia, flew frequent training missions over the Sea of Japan. Their Z-9 helicopter was on a routine training flight, and Dai was banking on routine, hoping they would be slack in terms of monitoring any real threats. Certainly, the aircraft out of Okinawa were not seen as a threat due to the detente between China and the US, a critical trading relationship.

However, Dai had not counted on the quick thinking of Lieutenant Gregory Marston. Marston had been momentarily stunned when his throttle jammed and then further alarmed when the ailerons would not respond. He watched in horror as the Chinese helicopter came into his path. Cursing the oblivious pilot of the helicopter, he killed all power to his craft. He could only pray it lost altitude and thrust quickly enough to allow the Chinese pilot to get out of the way. He barely heard Jeff Rawls, his co-pilot, as he frantically called in a Mayday to Futenma while simultaneously ejecting a flare to alert the Chinese pilot to take evasive action. Both men braced for impact as the Osprey crashed into the sea. After the Mayday call, his fellow Marines would be on their way to the rescue by the time they hit the first wave.

Marston and Rawls released the safety catches on their windows and maneuvered out of the Osprey and onto the wings. Designed to float for ten minutes even in seas of 8-10-foot waves and wind speeds of 28-40 knots, the Osprey was designed to provide an extra margin of safety. The relative flat sea and calm winds would assure a longer period of flotation. Even so, they anxiously watched the minutes tick by. Unless help arrived soon, they would be in the water.

"Nice day for a swim if all else fails," Marston called.

Rawls looked over at his companion and shouted across the fuselage, "What the hell just happened?"

"Damned if I know. Everything was copasetic and then I couldn't get the bird to respond to my commands. All I can think is that it was some kind of computer glitch that shut down part of the controls."

"Boy, we will be in for a grilling when we get back to base. Let's just be glad we didn't hit the Chink."

Marston sat up and strained his ears, "Oh, crap. I suspect that boat I hear is not one of ours."

"Hell. This is not going to be fun."

Marston squinted at the sea as the speck on the horizon drew ever nearer. "Yeah, that's the Chinese Coast Guard's Type-528 reconnaissance boat. Thankfully, at 13 meters it's too small to do anything about our bird."

Rawls and Marston watched the Chinese patrol boat maneuver to come alongside the downed craft. Momentarily Marston regretted he had not triggered the automatic destruct device to keep his Stealth from falling in Chinese hands. He could only pray the marines arrived in time to snag his bird if it continued to float and before a Chinese towboat came to recover it.

"Well Rawls, it looks like we are going to be guests of the CCG judging by the way that guy is waving his machine gun."

"Sure as hell looks that way."

Both men stood up with hands raised overhead as they waited to see what would happen. It didn't take long for the man in the bow of the boat to toss a rope and mime to Rawls to tie it around his waist and swim to the boat. Now another machine gun was aimed in their direction.

"Looks like you go first, buddy. Unless they shoot me, they'll be inviting me to swim over, too."

Rawls snorted, "Not very friendly acting, are they?"

Marston watched as his co-pilot tied himself to the rope and then jumped into the water. He couldn't decide if he were swimming to the boat or if the Chinese were pulling him. Once that was done, the overweight man in the bow motioned for him to climb over the fuselage to their side of the craft. Again the rope was tossed and Marston repeated the trip Rawls had made. The crew did not wait for him to climb in but reached down and yanked him over the gunnels.

When he settled in beside his co-pilot, both men looked up at the sound of another Stealth flying low overhead. The Chinese said something and laughed.

Rawls grinned, "Wish we spoke Chinese, but I doubt we would enjoy what they're laughing about. Hey, you guys, want to share the joke. We could use a laugh about now."

Their captors met the comment with stern silence.

Rawls chuckled. "Oh well, it's their party not ours."

Marston muttered, "The Stealth spotted us so they know we've been picked up by the Chinese. Now let's hope our boys get on the horn and get us out of this mess. As close as we came to that damned helicopter, the PLAFF may try to say we were up to no good."

"Shit, Marston, that's no way to cheer me up." Rawls winked, "Got any dirty jokes to share?"

One of the men with a machine gun waved it at them and motioned for them to shut up. Marston shrugged his shoulders. Resigned to their predicament, he leaned back against the side of the boat, stretched out his legs, closed his eyes and settled in for a rest. Not knowing what they were facing, Rawls decided he should do the same. Neither man slept for worry about what the Chinese might do, and concern that they would snag the Osprey before their guys could retrieve it. As it was, they were lucky that the boat that picked them up was too small to tow their craft.

Marston was tired. He had been up late the night before Skyping with his parents and teenage sister. The news of this would hit them hard, and with his father recovering from a recent heart attack, he could only hope that the whole mess blew over and he was back on base before they learned anything of it. He smiled at the memory of their faces as they blew him good-bye kisses before logging off.

He opened his eyes as the engine slowed speed. Quite a reception appeared to await their arrival. He could only stare in awe as he considered how quickly the Chinese had managed to gather the large crowd. Off to the side he noted the harbor police and a number of men in various military uniforms. It did not look like a cordial reception committee. In minutes they would be docking under the lens of waiting photographers who were pressing up near the cordoned off area at the foot of the dock. So much for this being kept quiet. Marston nudged Rawls in the elbow.

His co-pilot opened his eyes and sat up. He whistled softly under his breath before glancing at Marston and mouthing, "Good luck, buddy."

Marston responded with a nod and signaled 'you, too.'

As the boat nudged the dock, one of the men onboard tossed a line to a man standing on the dock who tied it to the cleat, then motioned the two Americans to get out of the boat. A harsh command from the fat guy with a machine gun, that had glared at them most of the way, had both Rawls and Marston scrambling onto the dock. Two of the harbor police, pistols drawn and expressions grim, marched down to where they were standing. Behind them they could hear the engine rev as the boat pulled away to resume patrol.

With a pistol prodding each of their backs, they began to march toward the quayside.

Rawls mumbled, "Well, at least we don't have to deal with Porky Pig anymore."

The policeman that was keeping step with him growled, "Chinese not pig. You find out. Now shut mouth."

"No offense, man. I wasn't referring to you."

"I say shut mouth."

Marston and Rawls followed the policeman that stepped in front to lead them, aware at every step of the guns aimed at their backs. Approaching a grim looking cement building with a steel door and barred windows, their destination became apparent. As they neared, the door swung open on grating hinges, and they were motioned in. The two harbor police stayed outside. It didn't matter. Two more men with guns were awaiting them inside a small room containing two chairs behind a steel table and two stools in front of it. The two men took their seats behind the table and motioned their prisoners to the stools.

Marston didn't wait for them to begin. "Do either of you speak English, if not I request an interpreter, please."

"We both speak English which would be unnecessary if you arrogant Americans would learn to speak something besides English." The man on the right, obviously of superior rank judging by the uniform, slowly crossed his arms in front of him as he studied the two men.

Again, Marston hastened to speak, "There has been a terrible misunderstanding. We were flying well within non-territorial boundaries when our plane stopped responding to our command. To avoid crashing into one of your choppers, we deliberately crashed into the sea. Rather than treating us like criminals, you should be thanking us that we went to great pains and considerable cost to our government to avoid a collision with your craft."

"We will determine whether or not you are criminals." The officer shuffled papers and picked up a pen, "Your names? Unit? Where are you stationed?"

Marston gave their names and rank and the station on Okinawa, then asked questions of his own. "I want to contact the American Consul in Shanghai. Could you tell me where we are?"

"This is Haizhi Port. We are not far from Shanghai. I have no permission to allow you a telephone until my commander questions you. You will be taken to Shanghai for investigation. You ask him then."

For the next hour, Marston repeated the same answers and Rawls corroborated them when it was his turn. When it was apparent they would learn no more, the junior officer who had done the questioning picked up his papers and followed his superior from the room. The only thing the superior ranking officer said was in Chinese. The two airmen did not have long to wonder what he had said as they were locked in the barren office with no idea what to expect next.

Chapter 5

After three days of no further response, Quint left the hospital and drove to his home on Park Drive. If nothing else, he planned to take a long shower and sleep in his own bed for the first time in weeks. As for the clothes he had been wearing, he stepped out of his shower an hour later and looked at the pile they made on the tile floor. He hesitated only a moment before scooping them up and carrying them to the garbage bin in his garage. That done he walked back to his bedroom, peeled back the covers of his bed, and was soon deep in sleep. His body was far more tired than he could ever remember. The uncomfortable and tedious hospital room was made even more frustrating by Lila's continuing coma. His last thought before sleep overtook him was to question what to do next. Was it any use to continue endless days sitting by her beside and talking until he grew hoarse and then continuing until words failed him? Was there anything he could do to find what had caused the accident that his friends and cohorts in the CIA were not already doing?

The sun had long since risen when Quint opened his eyes. For a moment he was disoriented. Remembering where he was, he threw back the covers and went to his bathroom to shower and shave. Looking in the mirror at a face that was pleasant without being strikingly handsome he shrugged at himself. After throwing on a fresh pair of jeans and an oxford shirt, Quint accessed his carefully built basement office through a secret panel that hid a narrow stairway down. Logging into his CIA direct account, he checked emails and company chatter. Most of it was routine and did little to excite his interest. Bored with the chore, he decided to leave the last dozen or so until later. First he wanted to call Figure Eight, talk to his housekeeper, and check on Code. He missed the dog badly. It was the longest he had ever been away from him and he worried what effect it would have on Code. He smiled as he pictured him cavorting on the beach as he chased sand fiddlers. With the call behind him, he gathered the few things he would take to the hospital for his continued vigil, before locking the house and securing the various alarms that made his Raleigh residence as impregnable as a fortress.

He walked into the hospital, pausing to speak to the various staff members who were well acquainted with him after his weeks there. A couple of the nurses gave him lingering looks as though they would like to pursue a flirtation, but he ignored them as he walked past the nurses' station to Lila's room. He walked into the darkened room lit only by the blinking monitors, stashed his bag in the locker beside the bed, and walked over to open the blind. When he turned back to the bed, he met Lila's eyes.

Shaking his head in disbelief he approached the bed to see if she had in truth emerged from her coma. Carefully, he lifted her hand to avoid disturbing any intravenous lines that might hurt her and squeezed it gently. "Are you really awake, darling?"

Lila blinked once before closing her eyes. Using his foot, he dragged a chair to the bedside without letting go of her hand. Once again, he began the daily spew of words. "I am so happy you are waking up darling. You have slept a long time, and I have been so worried. You know I love you and I need you. I want so much for you to be better so we can go forward with our lives. Open your eyes again, baby. Talk to me if you can."

After an hour with no response from the comatose woman, he was beginning to run out of words and again despair hovered around him in the room. He stood up and walked to the window and was staring unseeing into the parking lot when a soft noise from behind him caused him to turn back to the bed. Lila's eyes were open and watching him. A faint smile tugged at her lips. Quint broke into a huge grin as he hurried back to the bed.

"Thank God, baby. You have been sleeping long enough. Please try to stay awake for me."

Lila struggled to talk, managing to croak, "Thirsty…"

Filling a cup from the bedside tray, he stuck a straw in it and held it to her lips as she slowly sipped, her eyes never leaving him. She nodded her head slightly when she had finished and sighed.

"What happened?" Her voice was rusty from lack of use. There was no mistaking the alarm in her eyes as she looked around the room and realized where she was.

"There was an accident while you were driving to Figure Eight. I was waiting for you and when you didn't come, I started calling. With Gerald's help, I was able to track you to Rex Hospital. You have been in a coma for almost two weeks. I have been so worried, but now that you have regained consciousness, you're going to be fine."

"Am I hurt?" She looked puzzled when she asked.

"You had a bad concussion, but you are going to be okay now. And you have a passel of bruises, but no broken bones. The doctor should be here soon. He is going to be nearly as happy as I am to see you awake."

Lila nodded her head and closed her eyes.

"Try to stay awake, Lila."

"I'm not sleeping. I'm just resting my eyes." Lila gave a faint smile, "Bet you think I've rested them long enough."

Quint laughed and it felt good. "Yeah, I damned well do. If you will open them again, there is something I've been meaning to ask you."

Lila squinted at him, "What's that?"

"I've never done this before and never envisioned doing it in a hospital room, but here goes." Quint squeezed her hand, "Lila, would you do me the honor of marrying me. I love you, babe, and I want to be with you always."

"I suspect I might, but we need to settle some things first." Lila winked at him, "For instance, just because I agree to marry you it doesn't give you the right to boss me around. I intend to go on doing what I do for the CIA."

"What you do for the CIA almost got you killed. I don't want the mother of my children risking her life this way."

"O for Pete's sake, Quint. We don't have children, so let's save this argument for later."

Quint switched the subject to talk about the news and items of interest she had missed during the time she was in a coma. Whenever, her eyes began to close, he would ask her a question.

It was during one of her responses to his question that Smithson knocked on the open door and walked into the room. When he saw Lila with open eyes and talking, he beamed. "This just made my day. So, when did you wake up, Miss Bright Eyes?"

"How long has it been, Quint?"

"Almost an hour." Quint grinned at the doctor, "I think she just agreed to marry me. So, how about getting her well so we can get out of here?"

"I conditionally agreed," Lila chided but she, too, was smiling.

"She's cantankerous as all heck. But I love her anyway."

"You certainly didn't waste any time, Quint. Congratulations, you two. Lila, you've got a good man here. He's been with you night and day. I was afraid that chair was going to adhere to his backside. Now, let's check you out and see how you're doing."

While the doctor was with Lila, Quint walked down the hall and called Gerald to let him know that Lila had come out of the coma. He promised to question her about the accident details as soon as the doctor thought it was okay. He ended the call and stuck the phone back in his pocket. He was leaning against the wall propped on one foot, when Smithson emerged and saw him waiting.

"That is one tough and lucky woman. All of her vitals look good, so I'm removing the PIC-line and catheter. We will ease into a regular diet, but she can shower and go to the bathroom. That will help her feel more normal. I suspect she will experience some memory gaps for a while. I'll have a therapist work with her so we can assess if there is any long-term brain damage. We are going to get her up and walking sometime today. She may be a little shaky at first after so long in bed. The leg massages and exercises we gave her while she was in the coma should have helped prevent too much muscular atrophy, though. But, on the whole, I would say she has turned the corner and is going to be fine. You have been a real trooper, Quint. I know it has not been easy for you."

"Thank you for everything, Doc. I am so relieved!"

"So am I. I was beginning to be more than a little concerned." Smithson slapped him on the back, "Now, on to the next patient.

I'd love to get some good news there, too."

Day-by-day Lila grew stronger, and with Quint by her side encouraging her, she was well on the way to discharge. Despite Gerald's constant harping on the need to question her further about the accident, Quint resisted as the subject seemed to agitate her. Whenever he mentioned it, she immediately shut down and said she was tired. The therapist provided little help. She said with brain injuries the patient frequently found remembering painful and thus blocked anything that caused them to relive the moment of trauma. The only thing that he could take comfort in was assurances from every corner that she would fully recover. As for Lila, the stronger she became, the more remote she seemed. After two days of relative silence or brusque replies, Quint decided he had had enough.

Although he left nightly now to go home to sleep, he spent fourteen hours or more daily in her room. They both needed a break. Quint took a deep breath, "Lila, I have some business I need to take care of. I may be gone for a few days. You are going to be fine and you don't need me hovering over you every minute."

"I know I'm being a bitch. But I beg you Quint don't leave me. I'm scared."

"What are you scared of, Lila. You're safe here."

"You don't get it, do you? This accident damned well didn't happen because of something I did to cause it."

"Then for God's sake tell me what did happen."

"I don't know."

"Lila, if you don't know how do you know you didn't cause it?"

"Because I can remember everything was going fine until suddenly it seemed as though the car wouldn't respond. I remember I couldn't steer as nothing I did changed the direction of the car. I tried to put on brakes, and they didn't work. I remember approaching a curve, and in desperation I turned off the ignition, but it was too late. I remember going off the road and then everything went black."

"What do you think happened?"

"The hackers found me first. They know who I am, and they tried to kill me so I couldn't nail them. As soon as I get out of this hospital, I'm going after them."

"The hell you are!" Quint glared at her. "You've done enough. I'm taking you to Figure Eight the minute you're discharged, and you're staying there. While you are there, you need to set up a totally new IP address for both of us. If this jerk hacked into you and got all your info, chances are he has compromised not only you, but everyone in your contact list."

"Oh, no! Gerald!"

"Yes, Gerald. The Agency, too. From what Gerald says they have already shut down your system so there is no longer an interface. They have morphed into a new protocol that should protect them for awhile. This whole internet thing has become a constantly shifting game of trying to stay ahead of the hackers. It looks as though you ran across one of the better ones and pissed him off."

"I am going to chase that asshole until I nail him. He can't do this to me and just go laughing into the sunset."

"Don't worry. He's not going to mess with someone I love and get away with it. I have already told Gerald he had damned well better assign me to the case, because one way or another, I'm going to stop the son of a bitch."

"Not without me! Besides your expertise is in cracking codes, not hacking into computers." Lila glared at him and he glared back.

Suddenly she laughed, "Oh, for goodness sake, Quint, give it a rest. It's not like I can do anything at the moment except try to get out of here.

Quint was unwilling to concede to her. There was no way she was going to get back in the middle of this one even if he had to tie her down and cut the electricity to his beach house. "Just get well. We can settle this later."

"Could you kiss me, please," Lila asked in a small little girl voice.

Quint obliged. "Poor baby, stop being so tough and let me take care of you for once."

"Dammit, don't patronize me. We both know I can run circles around you on the computer. If this guy could get to me, what makes you think you can outsmart him?" Lila grimaced, "Look, I don't mean you're stupid or anything. You're smart as all hell. But, this is my turf. It's what I do. I found him once, and I can find him again. I just have to be patient and wait for him to make a mistake. And now that I know what kind of asshole I'm dealing with, I'll be a lot more careful. The rest of it is up to you and Gerald to deal with."

"I'm tired, Lila. I'm going to my house, take a long hot shower, and sleep in a decent bed. I'll be back in the morning. The nurse will be here soon to take you for a walk. Then I want you to eat a good dinner. Now, you give me a kiss and behave yourself."

Chapter 6

Lieutenant Gregory Marston leaned back in his chair in exhaustion. He and his co-pilot, Jeff Rawls had endured five hours of hostile Chinese interrogation before being turned over to the custody of the US consulate in Singapore. It was not long before they found themselves back on the island of Futenma at their home base and again being interrogated. He glared at the man across from him, Major John Roberts, an arrogant son-of-a-bitch if there ever was one. Delegated by the commanding general, James Dickson, Roberts was zealous in his questioning of the two airmen. Marston figured he was out to earn a higher rank by busting the asses of Rawls and himself. Hell, he'd probably climb over Christ almighty if it would help his career. He studied the major from his carefully combed but thinning hair to the immaculate uniform. Roberts would be considered handsome by women, he supposed, but there was a cold calculation about him that Marston found unsettling. He didn't know it, but Roberts hated his job.

The major hated being stationed in Japan. He hated the self-assurance of the two men sitting in front of him. He should not be serving in some out of the way backwater. He belonged in the Pentagon among the decision makers. He had been raised in a family of military men who had used their positions to gain public attention and then public office. His father had risen to Senator. His grandfather was a well-remembered governor and his grandfather had been an ambassador. He glowered at Marston and Rawls as though he blamed them for his lowly status.

Marston could not prevent the exasperated tone of his voice when he replied, "I can't tell you any more than I already told the Chinese guys. We lost control of the bird. It was like suddenly nothing responded to our commands. Pull the damned on-board computer and see what it shows."

"Lieutenant Marston, do not get smart with me. Just answer my questions." Roberts skewered him with a steely stare. "Now, let's start again. According to protocol, you are ordered to destroy a ditched craft, if possible, to prevent it and the onboard technology from falling into enemy hands. You did not follow procedure. Why not?"

"Sir, we had just flown over one of our own ships and assumed it would reach us long before any Chinese. We did not realize there was a CCG boat approaching from the other direction. As you know, they were too small to do anything more than capture us. We figured that our ship would recover the bird before the Chinese could get anywhere near it. Plus, one of our birds spotted us right after we went down. Not only that, but we had little time to do more than radio for rescue after we dodged the Chinese helicopter. I should think you would be grateful we didn't crash into the damned thing; that you still have our bird; and the Chinese did not continue to blame us for trying to cause some kind of incident."

"At this point, we have yet to determine if it was your error that caused what could have been a major embarrassment for the US government, and a potential harm to our relationship with the Chinese." Roberts glanced in front of him at the papers on the desk. He shuffled the top one aside and studied the second before asking, "Captain Rawls, did you make any attempt to assist Marston in avoiding the crash, before you put out the mayday?"

"In all due respect, sir, Lieutenant Marston is a superb pilot. I saw what was happening when nothing responded on the bird, and I called mayday as ordered. We anticipated a quick pick-up from our guys. Neither one of us had any reason to believe the Chinese would reach us first, and it would have been a shame to destroy a valuable aircraft needlessly."

"Neither one of you had any reason to think what was or was not needless when procedures have been drilled into you both."

Rawls cracked, "Well, Major, it makes me think you are sorry the bird didn't sink."

"One more comment like that and you'll be in the brig."

Both Marston and Rawls stared at Roberts. Neither felt the need to add anything more. Marston felt sweat run down his armpits and suspected Rawls was equally uncomfortable.

Roberts shuffled his papers into a stack and then glanced back at them. "The President is aware of this incident and very alarmed at the potential international ramifications of it. I suspect he will be sending someone for further questioning on this. Until, that time, you are both confined to base per General Dickson's personal orders. If it were left up to me, you would both be in the brig. Best keep your noses clean. Do you understand?"

"No problem, sir. It's not exactly like we have anywhere to go," Marston snapped.

"Don't get smart with me, Lieutenant."

"No, sir."

"You're dismissed. Now get the hell out of here."

Marston and Rawls walked from the office into the bright

morning sunshine that helped offset a cold wind. Rawls zipped up his flight jacket and chuckled, "I guess he didn't get any this morning from that piece of ass everybody says he's been banging."

"Whatever. He is one miserable asshole to deal with. I suspect we will be old men long before anyone bothers to thank us for avoiding a real mess and saving our Osprey."

"Since we won't be flying anytime soon, care for a beer and a game of pool?"

"Rawls, I think that is a damned stellar idea. But, no betting. I've learned my lesson. I'm tired of you winning all of my extra cash."

"Aw, come on be a sport. What's a little matter of money among friends?"

"Forget it. You want to bet, choose another sucker."

"You drive a hard bargain. Yeah, no betting." Rawls paused, "Hey, Marston, what in the hell did happen? I know we did everything we could and nothing responded. That bird never acted like that before." It's enough to freak me out.

"I don't know either, but I certainly intend to keep the pressure on until someone finds out."

"How are you going to do that? Your dad connected or something?"

"Nope, but I'm going to figure something out."

"Good luck, buddy. If there was something wrong with the bird, our mechanics will figure it out. If it was a computer glitch, we got guys for that, too. We don't either one have that kind of expertise in computer software. Hardware either for that matter. We just fly the damned things."

"Yeah, I know. It's just frustrating as all hell not to be able to do something about it, especially when we're getting our asses chewed through no fault of our own."

"Tell me about it." Rawls slapped Marston on the back as they entered the bar. "I'll stand the best pilot I know to a beer, if you'll stand the best co-pilot you know to the next one."

Marston made a great show of looking around. "Gee, I don't see him."

Rawls chuckled, "Screw you." Both men laughed as they headed to the bar.

*****

Dai was not laughing. He had counted on a major incident that would create hostility between the United States and China, one that would chill the warming relationship between the two countries. He leaned back in his chair and worked his tongue around his mouth to clean the debris sticking to his teeth after a recent lunch. He stared at his computer screen without seeing it as he ran options through his mind. The next plan had to work. After twenty minutes of intense concentration, he sat up and began typing.

Pong Ju's face filled the screen. Immediately, Dai demanded, "Do you have the information I asked you to get?"

"I do, but I don't like how I got it. I used a friend of mine. I got him drunk and asked him questions. He answered them. Later he came to me very upset that he had given me secret information. I'm afraid he could report me if something goes wrong."

"He wouldn't dare as he would then incriminate himself." Dai's voice softened with feigned sympathy, "Who is this friend of yours and what does he do?"

Pong Ju hesitated before responding, "He works for the

missile development program in Yongbyon. He knew the things I asked for. When he sobered up he must have wondered why I would want to know. His superiors will kill him if they discovered the secrets he divulged."

"I understand. Now, who is he?"

Again, Pong Ju was wary of answering. He looked at Dai's face on his computer screen and took a deep breath. The Chinaman owned him now; he could either continue to collude with him, or he would die. "He is Rhee Chae-Won. He has computer access to everything about the missile program."

"Find out where he lives. I want the names of those in his family. Learn his daily routine. If necessary, we can protect you if we know these things."

"He lives near me. It will be easy to get all you want to know."

Dai continued to question Pong Ju about what he had learned. When he was satisfied, he had everything he needed for his next plan, he ended the session with Pong Ju. This next project would be seen as either ineptitude on the part of the North Koreans or an unprovoked attacked on a US ally. Either way it would send a lot of governments scrambling in panic. He would then again turn his attention to China. Perhaps, it was best to keep things random rather than focused on one entity.

*****

The residents of the coastal Japanese village of Kamala began their daily routine the same as they had done for centuries. It was a life devoted to fishing. Directly or indirectly every person in town was tied to the success or failure of the daily catch. Their day began before dawn as men ate a hasty breakfast and picked up their lunch bags before kissing their wives goodbye and heading to the harbor. In the homes they had vacated, their wives were beginning to awaken children and help them dress for the school day. The sun rose as it had done since the beginning of time, birds chirped in the trees, shadows from trees and buildings crept across the village, and from countless backyard pens roosters announced the beginning of a new day. Neither animal nor human would see another sunrise.

Originally aimed at a point in the Sea of Japan, North Korea's test missile veered from its planned trajectory and flew onward carrying its burden of death to an unsuspecting populace. The village's only survivors were the fishermen who had already departed for the sea. Later some of them would die at their own hands as they could not cope with a life devoid of friends, and family…homes, wives, children, mothers, fathers, brothers, sisters, aunts, uncles, and cousins…all destroyed in the space of seconds. Life as they had known it in all its simplicity and comfort vanished in a column of deadly fire.

The world reeled at the implications of the attack. North Korea protested its innocence of intent and pledged financial compensation. The UN called a special session. The President of the United States sent the ambassador to Japan to meet with its leaders. Gerald Williams, Director of the CIA, began calling operatives in various Asian countries. The world held its collective breath as it struggled to deal with another deadly peril.

Marston and Rawls had just finished their third beer and were watching the small television above the bar, when a newsflash interrupted regular programming. As the announcer began to detail the destruction of a small Japanese fishing village by a North Korean missile, both men sat forward in their chairs.

"Damn, Rawls. We are in the middle of one can of worms now. My God, it could just as well have been this base they took out." Later the conversation would come back to haunt him like a bad echo.

"The Koreans say they had nothing to do with it. According to them, the missile suddenly went out of control."

"Wasn't there a ferry wreck not long ago near Phongyang where the Captain swore the same thing about his ferry? If there is some connection, we make three. I wonder if someone is playing God out there."

"More like the fucking Devil!"

Gerald Williams was thinking the same thing. There were too many incidences, too close together, to be mere coincidence. Somewhere one mean son-of-a-bitch was playing deadly games. If connected, Lila's made four cases of loss of control. He wondered if the same guy that had caused her car to crash could be behind the others. Minutes after the Japanese tragedy hit the airwaves, he had shared his concerns with the President in an emergency meeting. His assignment was to figure out whether the events were accidents or planned carnage. If deliberate, it was going to be imperative to find the perpetrator before he could trigger worldwide chaos. He needed Lila back on task. There was no way Quint would allow it unless they could establish failsafe security for her.

Chapter 7

Quint and Lila were lying in a pool of sweat after a vigorous session of lovemaking. Through the opening in the drapes, the ocean glistened beneath a hot sun. The breeze from the water moved the drapery in a listless flutter. Quint stirred restlessly but slept on for a few minutes more. Code lay beside the bed with his head resting on his front paws. He was happy to have his owner home again. Suddenly he lifted his head and growled low in his throat. Quint sat up, "Shhh, boy. Lila needs to sleep. That's just the repairman come to fix this air conditioning system before we all melt."

He eased from the bed. Reaching for his clothes, he struggled to pull a pair of wet bathing trunks onto his sweaty, damp body. They had been for a swim to cool off before going to the bedroom. In the heat and humidity, the trunks had not even begun to dry out. The weather was unseasonably hot for late October, and the ocean had not yet cooled to the uncomfortable cold of winter. Once he pointed the repairman in the right direction, he planned to go for another swim. He hoped Lila would sleep for a while longer. Only a week out of the hospital, she still tired easily. He felt momentary guilt that he had made love to her. After a long abstinence, they had both been ravenous…she as much as he, but that did not take away his unease that he should have waited until she grew stronger.

Lila murmured from the bed, "Whew, it's hot as hell in here."

"Maybe it won't be too much longer. The repairman just drove up. I'm going to get him started and then go for a swim to cool off."

"Were you just going to leave me here in misery?"

"I thought you needed to rest. That was quite a workout we just had."

"Mmmm, come back to bed and let's do it again."

"Later, you little hussy. Right now, I want some cool air coming out of those vents."

"Oh, well. I think I'll crawl back in my suit and join you for that swim." The sheet slipped from her nude body as she sat up. He looked away before he could be tempted to forget all else.

"I'll have Teresa make us a nice pitcher of lemonade. It should be waiting by the time you get to the kitchen."

Lila beamed, "Have I told you how wonderful that woman is? She is one more reason I love it here."

Quint and Code both turned at the sound of the doorbell. "Gotta go." Code followed him to the front door where he gave the repairman a once over before moving aside so the man could enter. After Quint had shown him the air conditioning units, Lila walked out dressed for the expected swim. He instantly hated the man when he saw the sudden flare of interest in the man's eyes. Quint took her hand. Staking his claim, he asked, "Ready for the beach, darling?"

He didn't wait for her reply. He grabbed her hand and towed her after him down to the sparkling surf. Teresa watched the whole interplay from her post by the kitchen door. Shaking her head with amusement, she began to prepare lunch. They would be hungry after their swim and judging by the sparks flying last night and the missed breakfast, she suspected they had an additional reason to be starved.

Two hours later, the system was pumping cold air, the house was cooling, and both Lila and Quint, showered and dressed, were waiting at the table by the window overlooking the ocean praying lunch would be soon. They were starving.

When Teresa sat the plates in front of them, Lila gasped, "Good grief, you should have been an artist. If this tastes anything like it looks, it will be to die for."

Looking at the plate, Quint could only agree. It was a beautiful presentation. Sautéed chunks of crispy grouper sat atop black beans that had been drained, partially mashed, and cooked with scallions, jalapenos and sweet red pepper. Around the bed of beans were concentric circles of finely minced parsley, fresh diced tomatoes, and chopped scallions. "Hold everything. I'm taking a picture of this. Wow, Teresa, this looks wonderful."

She made no comment as she waited for them to take their first bite. Eyeing the blissful looks on both faces, she smiled and walked back to the kitchen where her own plate awaited, along with a glass of perfectly chilled Pinot Grigio from the bottle they were enjoying. As she enjoyed her lunch, she could only send up a prayer of thanksgiving for the circuitous circumstances that led to her employment by Quint. She had grown to love him like a son. Lila she liked on first sight. She mused to herself that her lonely Quint was the happiest she had ever seen him. That alone was enough for her to love Lila. The phone on the kitchen counter rang insistently. Teresa picked it up so it would not interrupt her two love birds. "Cord residence. Who's calling, please?"

"Teresa, this is Gerald Williams. Could you get Quint on the phone without letting him know I am the one calling?"

"Yes, sir, I believe so. Just hold on."

Teresa approached the couple as they broke from a kiss. "Excuse me, Quint. The guy from the air conditioning company needs to talk to you. I have him on the phone in the kitchen."

Lila stood up, "Take it. I'm going to have a shower and put on something cool and dry."

Quint was unprepared to hear Gerald's voice on the line. "What's up? Why didn't you call me on my cell?"

"I was hoping to talk to you without Lila knowing. I'm not sure I want her to know how I might need your help on this. Grab your cell phone and walk down to the beach so we can talk without her hearing you."

"Sure. Give me a second."

As Gerald detailed recent incidents in Asia and the common thread of loss of navigational control, Quint walked along the wet sand just beyond the reach of the outgoing tide. Quint suspected that Lila's own accident might be a part of the same mystery. Without stating as much, it was obvious that Gerald's suspicions ran along the same lines.

Quint kicked at a glistening black form in the sand. Bending down he picked up a large shark tooth fossil. Polishing off the sand he dropped it in the pocket of his shorts. "I don't think you are telling me all of this just to have a conversation. So, what exactly is it you want from me?"

"I believe you told me you speak several languages. Want to tell me again what they are?" Gerald had his file in front of him and knew without asking.

"What? That came out of left field?"

"Yeah, yeah. So which ones do you speak?"

"I'm fluent in French and Italian. I can speak a little Spanish and German." Quint paused, "Oh, I almost forgot. I speak some

Japanese. Why?"

"I'm thinking of sending you fishing in China."

"I don't want to go fishing in China. I can catch fish all day long right out of my front yard." Quint suspected what Gerald was asking of him, but he wasn't going to make it any easier.

"Quint, before the accident Lila was tracking some asshole in China. He threatened her and suddenly her car goes out of control. Suppose he got into the computer system of her car and caused her to run off the road. Wouldn't you like to bring him to justice for causing so much harm?"

"You surely know the buttons to punch. So, how do you propose I do that? She's the computer expert, not me. And, I don't want her anywhere near China."

"Nor do I. She can work from here."

"I don't want her doing that. I don't want her to touch anything to do with this mess. She already nearly died. I think that's more than enough."

"Look, you've got a bunker there as secure as anything in Washington. I can set up a security detail like we did once before with drone surveillance and round the clock guards. I'll make your house as secure as the White House. It helps that you are on a private island with a security gate and you have fortified your house like Fort Knox. Lila will be fine. I'll put Buster on it."

Buster Walton, a former Seal, ran his own security firm that Gerald used for special cases. Quint liked Buster. Buster also liked Lila. That brought out a jealous streak that Quint could not admit to. Buster's interest in Lila overrode Quint's confidence in him. "I don't think that's a good idea. Buster is no computer expert, so what good is Buster if the guy can break into the computer of her car?"

"Lila is not going to be driving a car again until we catch this nut job. She won't like it, but we're planning to lock her up tight until we catch him."

"Good luck with that! She's as independent as all hell. I look forward to hearing her response when you lay this one on her." Quint's laughter was harsh.

"As a matter of fact, I was hoping you would tell her."

"I'll just bet you were."

"Let me tell you the plan and then you can tell me what you think."

"Go for it, but you had better make it damned good."

"We want to set up a sham corporation under the title K. Ford Enterprises. Supposedly you are involved with high-tech privacy solutions for industry. Lila is your employee. You are a hardnosed money man that has looked at the idea of remote control of computerized transportation and have seen a way to make money…essentially, through a protection scam whereby governments and industries are held hostage for payments to provide protection from computer takeovers. You are totally apolitical and interested in only the money angle. You will convince the asshole of this so we can nail him. As it is, we don't have anything but suspicions."

Quint interrupted, "So, how is it that I am supposed to contact this guy when we don't even know who he is? Furthermore, if that is his angle he's not going to want to split the pie."

"If that is the case, you need to convince him you can make his pie even bigger and more profitable to him. As for finding him, that's where Lila comes in. She nailed him once. According to Jeffrey Knotts… you should remember him, he's the crippled guy that worked on the last case we had…the hacker has changed his IP address and Jeffrey can't find him. Since Lila found him once, she should be able to track him again. If we can find the area where he is, we can put out feelers that will get the two of you connected. For the moment, all we want you to do is be on call. Do you think Lila is ready to begin tracking again?"

"I know she is eager as all hell to catch the guy that almost killed her. I just have to figure out how to restrict her to just the computer chase angle. You have to figure out how to keep her safe."

"So, does that mean you're in?"

"I didn't say that. Let's see what Lila comes up with first. If she can chase him to a location without him picking up on her, then we can decide what to do next. "

"That's reasonable. We are going to work on your cover. As soon as we have the corporation in place and a new IP address for Lila tied to the bogus corporation, she can start tracking.

"Okay. I'm not saying anything to her until you get back to me with the new protocol. I intend to protect her as best I can. In the meantime, see what you can set up here through Buster. She's not doing anything until this island is as secure as Alcatraz."

"That works for me."

Quint was still holding his phone in his hand when Lila walked down to the beach.

She took one look at him and knew he was hiding something. "Yeah, something's up, so try telling me why you are looking so sheepish."

"Gerald wants to know if you are ready to try to ID the guy in China. His other tech guy has been unable to find him since the asshole has changed his IP address from the one he was using when you tracked him."

"No need to ask. You know I want to nail him."

"We are not taking any more chances on him getting to you. Gerald plans to send Buster and his crew down to provide security here."

Lila raised an eyebrow and smiled, "Oh, good. I do like Buster. Not only is he sexy as all hell but he's fun."

Quint made no comment.

Chapter 8

Just when Lila thought she had broken through, a jester popped up on her screen and the site went blank. She cursed under her breath. He had caught her trying to hack into his system and put up a block. Judging by the previous time she had tracked him, he would go to an alternate routing and different IP address. Frustrated she stood up and walked into the living room where Quint was talking quietly to Buster and two of his operatives. She knew they were planning to lock the place down from every direction. While the safety factor had definite appeal, the idea of being a virtual prisoner carried none.

The men glanced up as she walked over and immediately fell quiet. She could tell from Quint's face they had been talking about her. "So, you guys get my prisoner status all figured out?"

"What's that?" Buster asked innocently.

"You know: locking me in so I can't go anywhere. At least leave me enough privacy to go to the bathroom without a camera watching." She grinned, but they all could see there was no mirth behind it.

"Oh, come on, Lila. You're trying to spoil all my fun." Buster chuckled.

Quint glared at Buster, "You had better hope that's a joke, because you're talking to my future wife here."

"Guess you had better back off, Buster. I kinda like this jealous version of my boyfriend."

Quint growled, "You mean fiancée."

"Hmmm, did I accept? Right now, I'm having memory problems. It must have been the accident."

"Yeah, right." Quint smiled, "Look, I know this whole thing gives you the willies, but we want you safe this time. No more accidents. That SOB almost took you out once. We don't want him to even come near you again."

"Nor do I. By the way, I tracked him again but he caught on and put up a roadblock. I'm going to have to try another route and see if I can find where in Ether-land he's hiding now."

Lila wandered into the kitchen leaving the men to resume their planning. Dragging a stool from the counter, she watched Teresa chopping a mountain of vegetables. "I sure hope you enjoy cooking for that mob out there."

"It don't bother me any. It's not that much more work to cook for six than it is to cook for three." Teresa glanced up from her work, "Can I get you something, honey?"

"I'm just restless. I have been sitting too long at the computer and needed to take a break." Lila stood up and walked to the refrigerator. They sat in companionable silence for several minutes. The wheels in Lila's head were turning trying to figure out her next approach but nothing was coming to her. Sighing in frustration, she said, "I think I'll pour myself a glass of wine. Would you like one, too?"

Teresa shook her head. "Not now. I'll get one later. But, thanks for asking."

"Sure."

After pouring a glass of wine, Lila returned to Quint's office and her waiting computer. Sitting in front of the monitor, she took a sip and stared at the screen. Instead of canceling the current IP address, she decided to keep it as a decoy and create an entirely new one for tracking the Chinese hacker. An hour later she had the two addresses running, one on her old computer that she had wiped clean of any information and the other on the new CIA encrypted computer Buster had brought.

She began a patient fishing game. The guy was very good, but so was she. She would find him eventually.

*****

Pong Ju logged onto his computer and sent the information that Dai had demanded about the family and address of Rhee Chai-Won. He did not know what Dai would do with it but he knew that Dai would now control one more North Korean. Perhaps, he thought, Dai won't need me now that he has Rhee. With Rhee's access to the missile program, he was a more valuable asset in many ways.

As for Dai, he did not intend to let either man off his deadly hook. Pong Ju provided information on ships and aircraft and Rhee Chai-Won gave the needed entrée to the missile and nuclear warhead program. Dai smiled in satisfaction before sending an email to Rhee. If the man wanted to save his family, he would do as Dai wanted. If not, he and his family would die and he would find another. It was unfortunate that he did not have that same family leverage with Pong Ju. So far Pong Ju was cooperating. The minute he stopped or was no longer useful, he would be expendable.

Rhee responded quicker than he had hoped. Already vulnerable due to providing the details that allowed the hit on the Japanese village, he knew his life was worthless. His family was another matter. Dai wasted no time in requesting information on the next missile launch. He already had his destination in mind.

An hour later he had what he needed. The launch scheduled for the next day was supposed to be unarmed. Rhee would change that. Now, Dai needed to only await the launch.

The following morning, Rhee walked into the second room in his small apartment which contained an all-purpose living and cooking area. His wife had just finished nursing his first son and had placed him in his small cradle. His mother had made her the traditional seaweed soup to restore iron lost during pregnancy. At the births of his two daughters, she had been so angry that she refused to make it for her daughter-in-law as was traditional. He hoped the birth of a son would soften the relationship between his parents and the woman they scorned as a wife for having failed him prior to the birth of this long-awaited son. He picked up the packaged food he would take to work. This was the last time he would ever see his home or his family. For a moment his resolve failed him, and he stood helplessly. His wife looked up in puzzlement. Squaring his shoulders, he forced a smile onto his face. Not normally demonstrative, he hugged his wife and children goodbye before turning resolutely to the door. Reading the sadness in his face, his wife watched his retreating back with unease. A chill ran up her spine. Her nunji or intuition told her something was very wrong with her husband. He had been so happy after the birth of their boy that she could not fathom what had changed. She opened her mouth to call to her husband. The words died in her throat. Surely, she was overreacting. Rhee was a careful man and a dutiful husband. They enjoyed a good life, blessed with children that were smart and healthy with more food than many and a better home than most. She should not listen to the whispers of evil spirits.

Rhee would arm the missile, aimed at who knew what. His position was high enough up the chain of command that no one would question his orders. If they did, he was ready. He was clever enough to create a fake order and relay it through enough channels that it looked authentic. Once the missile was in the air, he would take his life. It did not occur to him to take his life first rather than doing as Dai had instructed. He was so accustomed to obedience that the idea of not obeying was a foreign concept. The only way to free himself and save his family was to die, and to do so in such a way that it appeared to be an accident. According to North Korean belief junche or a man's actions, and not God, controlled one's destiny. The moment he had drunkenly confided secrets to his one-time friend, he had determined his fate.

*****

Marston and Rawls were bored. The idleness mandated by Major Roberts weighed heavily. Earlier they had gone to a showing of American Sniper followed by a stop at the officer's club. After one too many beers, the two men walked to their quarters and crawled into bed. Their barracks lay on the edge of the base. They laughingly called it Outer Mongolia when first assigned there as it made for a long hike to any destination on base. After the drinks and the hike, they were soon asleep.

The US base at Futenma was lax. No problems had occurred and none were expected. It was only at the last minute, with a missile bearing down on them, that an alert radar monitor started beeping in alarm to signal an in-coming trajectile. The men on duty scrambled to activate the anti-missile system. They were in time to deflect the trajectory, but not to stop the hit. It scored a crippling blow to half of the base. Buildings were instantly ignited and sleeping marines were incinerated where they lay. With a death toll at 79…and slated to rise as many of those badly injured would die before another sunrise, it was a serious blow to the US. Marston and Rawls were among the lucky thanks to the barracks location they had previously spurned.

Both men sat up in bed. The loud explosion and instant blare of sirens announced a serious incident. Neither had any idea of what had occurred as they scurried to the window to look out. All power on base was down, but the gory red of the sky from the direction of the west side of the base told them all they needed to know. Both men scrambled into their clothes and met one another at the exit. Marston looked at Rawls and could see his friend was a stunned as he was.

Rawls gaped at the sky, "Damn man, what in the hell happened?"

"No idea. Let's go see what's going on and what they need us to do. This looks bad."

They watched as burning men ran from the nearest barracks. In the panic, the men had forgotten the rule of drop and roll. Marston started running and yelling, Rawls on his heels doing the same. "Drop to the ground and roll. Stop running."

A few men heard them and the words sank in. They dropped and rolled. By then, for many of them, the injuries were to grave for them to survive. Others writhed in agony at the unendurable pain. Rawls went to the man nearest to the burning building and tried to pick him up in order to move him further from the flames. He dropped him when he realized that his effort was only causing more pain as the man's flesh began to fall away. He stuttered an apology and went back where Marston was.

"Crap. I'll be damned if I know what to do." Rawls shook his head in shame.

"I don't either; so don't kick yourself. Your intentions were good. The problem is until the ambulances get here there isn't much we can either one do."

"I wonder if the hospital was hit?"

Marston jerked his thumb in the direction of the hospital, "Why don't we jog over there and see? Maybe we can drive ambulances or help out in some other way."

"Yeah. That's better than standing here doing nothing."

The walk to the hospital area was increasingly grim as the buildings they passed were burning and more badly injured men that had managed to escape lay on the ground, some dying and others in terrific pain. As they rounded the corner of the headquarters building which had also been badly damaged, they saw ahead a shell of the hospital. No one was going to offer any help from that quarter.

"My God, what are we going to do now? Someone besides us must have survived uninjured. The question is where are they and what are we going to do to help these men?" Marston walked further into the area between the hospital and headquarters. "Look, there is an ambulance. They have to have first aid stuff in there. Do you know how to do any?"

"If we can find pain killers, I can at least give some of these poor devils a shot to help."

"Good. Let's get on it and see what we have to work with. I'm going to use my cell phone and see if I can rouse anyone on base. If I can't, I'm going to call out and have help sent in. Hell, I'm going to call out period. This mess is bigger than we can handle."

In the ambulance they found hypodermics which Rawls began preparing while Marston called the outside world to alert others to the problem. When he reached the office in Singapore, they told them they had already had an alert from Japan that the base at Futenma had been hit. Quickly Marston filled them in on the damage and requested medical assistance for survivors. He turned to Rawls when he rang off, "It's up to us for the next little while to do what we can. Help is on the way, thank God, but it is going to be at least an hour before it gets here."

"Hey, you speak a little Japanese. See if you can get help from the local Japanese hospital in the meantime."

"Good idea. I'm on it. Now let's get this buggy rolling to the barracks area and see what we can do. Maybe some of the other guys from our barrack are around and can help us."

Rawls started the ambulance and headed for the barracks area. "There are only two other ambulances, but I guess if they will still go that's better than nothing. Did you see if the upper officer's area had been hit? Since they are close to us, they may have survived, too."

Marston shook his head. He had not looked any further once they discovered an unharmed ambulance. "Who knows? Apparently, my call was the first one to Singapore, so that doesn't sound good."

"Hey, I wondered if any of our birds survived."

"I have no idea. Right now, I'm going to do a search to see if I can find the local hospital number. As for birds, without men and backup crews, we are pretty much defunct."

Chapter 9

President Northrup looked around the table as each man turned to him. He held their eyes as he slowly made the circuit. Victor Erickson, DNI director fiddled with the papers arrayed before him. The new Vice-President, Derrick Taylor hastily named on the death of his predecessor, flicked constantly at this ball point pen. He nodded at the commander in charge of the Asian forces, General John Quinlan, who squirmed in his chair as his face slowly turned red. True to form, Director of the CIA, Gerald Williams snapped another pencil in half. The others in the room were equally uncomfortable.

"We have a situation here. This time it is not being pinned on us, but on the North Koreans. They swear they had nothing to do with the hit at Futenma. According to Kim Jong Un, the missile was just a routine test to determine range and was not meant to fly that far. It also was supposed to be unarmed. The Japanese are furious since the attack on Kamala and are mad as all hell that we didn't immediately blow the North Koreans out of the water. Our own military wants retaliation. China is dithering, unsure of which way to fall. South Korea is raising hell about Kim's entire missile program, saying it is even more problematic if they cannot even control a test. The UN is sitting on its collective thumb. The questions before us are: if the test was for range only, why was it armed: if it was not aimed at Futenma, why did it land there; and what do we do about it?

Northrup turned to the right and barked, "Director Williams, your opinion, sir."

Gerald pushed the detritus from the broken pencil to one side before thoughtfully answering, "Mr. President, my advice is to take the North Korean explanation at face value. I think this incident ties into the previous ones where there was an unexplained interference with the guidance system. Of course, that doesn't explain the armed warhead. I still advise restraint. At the moment, my tech people are trying to track some asshole in China that thinks he is a computer hotshot. They tend to think he might well be behind this."

"That's all well and good. The problem is the pressure to come up with something before the baying hounds run away with this. My press secretary has been beaten up by about every journalist in the room wanting to know why we haven't reacted, especially since North Korea is not noted for honesty."

General Quinlan snarled, "So, Mr. Williams, are we supposed to twiddle our thumbs and wait for another hit? The press is killing us."

Ignoring Quinlan, Gerald carefully laid the broken pencil on his notepad as he continued, "With all due respect, Mr. President, the media is not in charge of this country. What to do is ultimately your decision and one that needs to be based on real facts and not conjecture. I can understand the pressure you are under to act, believe me. Since it falls in my arena to find out what is behind this, I feel it, too. My techie is good. One of the best. She nailed him once but he got to her and damned near killed her as I told you. Since then, he has changed his IP address and is staying one skip ahead of her. She'll nail him again, but we need a little time."

The President gave none of the others time to respond.

"Gentlemen, you are dismissed. Mr. Williams, I would like a moment more with you."

An hour later, Gerald left the oval office feeling rung out. He wanted nothing more than a hot shower, a stiff Woodford Old Fashion, and to crawl in bed and cuddle his wife, Jill. That was an idle wish, and he knew it. Squaring his shoulders he left the White House for the ride back to his office. On the way, he called Jill to say he would be late for dinner.

Jill sighed and told him not to worry, she would keep it warm.

When he got to the office, he dialed Lila to tell her to put a rush on it.

She snorted at him. "Jesus, I'm doing all I know to do. This is not easy."

He stared through his office window at an angry sky. The distant rumble of thunder and a flash of lightening promised another storm. The fury of the coming storm seemed a metaphor for the situation in Asia. His gut told him a lone wolf operating with an unknown agenda was responsible for the series of incidents beginning with Lila's accident. The challenge was to stop him before he could trigger a major conflict and potentially a nuclear conflagration affecting the entire globe.

He accepted she was doing all she could and as rapidly as she could. But he had no choice but to urge haste. He walked back to his desk and sat in his chair hunching forward over the desk pad as they talked. Lila liked to work alone but he didn't have the luxury for that. The President was impatient for answers. After they hung up, he snapped another pencil in half. Knocking the pieces into the waste basket, he drummed his fingers for several minutes before reaching for his rolodex. Jeffrey Knotts had been a good field man before a bullet consigned him to his wheelchair for life. During his recovery he had studied computer science until he was an expert. He didn't have the intuitive talent of Lila, but he was very good. He had no choice but to call Jeffrey and explain the urgent need for answers and order him to gin up his own search for the culprit that Gerald was certain was behind all of the occurrences. Lila and Jeffrey agreed with him on that. Between the two, they had better find something before the President was forced to pull the trigger.

*****

Pong Ju spoke rapidly. With his throat clogged by tears, he was hard to understand.

Dai exhorted himself to patience despite a white-hot anger, "Tell me again why you have telephoned? You are well aware that I asked you to only contact me by email. We do not want our correspondence traced. When you email, I can hide it. It is more difficult for me to hide a call that goes through our company switchboards."

"I'm sorry. I forgot."

"Fine! Just don't do it again. Now tell me why you called me? And make it fast." He could not keep the impatience from his voice.

"I am reading today's Rodong Sinmun. That is the official Workers' Party newspaper..."

"I know what it is." Dai snapped. "Why is reading a newspaper so important that you must break my first rule?"

"It's Rhee Chae-won. He's dead. They say it was an accident, but I don't believe it. I think it was suicide, and we are responsible for his death. I should never have told you about him." Pong Ju hated the man on the other end of the line. He must have beidsun...tainted blood passed down from his forefathers from generation to generation. He could find no other explanation for the evil in Dai.

"Pull yourself together. Hang up so I can start trying to eradicate this call record. I will contact you later in the normal way. Remember: do not call me at my office again…ever!" Dai slammed the phone down.

Pong Ju could take no more. He was in over his head. Leaving the office for the day, he walked to the bus. Rusted and dilapidated from lack of maintenance, the bus was the only way for many to commute to work. Without a private car and no means to have one, he had no choice but to ride it or walk. He usually napped during the time it took to reach his home, but today he could only stare blankly ahead. There was no question in his mind that Dai was behind Rhee's suicide. He could only hope that the man's family would not be made to pay the price if the government realized what he had done. When he reached his bus stop, he walked down the aisle, and as though bent over from the weight of his decision, stepped to the pavement like someone who had aged thirty years in the fifty-minute ride. He looked around at the rough concrete buildings, the befouled streets, and the hungry people that slinked by…all as afraid as he was to meet anyone's eyes. The price of revenge had become too high for him to stay in this country that offered its people little beyond deprivation, fear, and pain.

Pong Ju's computer was beeping when he walked in. The image of Dai was in the corner of the screen that told him who was trying to access him. He did not hesitate. Walking to the wall, he yanked out the power cord and watched the screen go black. He was finished with Dai. Now he had two enemies, his country and the Chinaman. They would both try to kill him when they realized he was running.

Pah Pong Ju was not a stupid man, but he admitted to himself that he had been a naïve one when he allowed himself to be used by Chen Dai. It was not his original plan of revenge against Kim, but if he wanted to live, leaving his country was mandatory. He had no choice but to flee to the Chinese border and from there utilize the network through either China or Mongolia that helped defectors reach South Korea. He only hoped he had enough hidden in the lockbox under his bed to pay the bribes and fees it would cost. With his uncle's friends still in high offices, and with his job, he had access to channels of information denied to many of his countrymen. Despite the oppressive nature of the regime, he and many others knew of the efforts of Christian groups in Mongolia willing to help refugees gain access to South Korea. In China there were traffickers, who for a fee, would procure passports and any other papers needed to get to South Korea.

He studied the map and tried to determine the best point of entry. The people's grapevine, while based on hearsay, was the most reliable in a country where the government controlled all media. According to rumor the easiest was through Musen, a small town not far from the industrial city of Chongjin. From Musan, a trafficker would give him the route to the Tumen River and a point shallow enough to wade across to the rural Chinese countryside. A contact there would take him to Luguo Shangshazhou where he would be taken to a safe house while passports and documents were arranged to take him into North Korea either through China or Mongolia. On the other hand, the more direct route ran from Pyongyang to Sinuiju, across the Yalu River at Dandong, and then on to Dalian. Dalian, a Coastal Chinese seacoast resort lies directly across the Yellow Sea from

Korea. From its airport he could fly to the international Seoul airport of Incheon and claim refugee status.

He ran through a mental list of his father's friends who had survived the purge and could be trusted to help him. He rejected most of them one by one as they were the types that would be too fearful to involve themselves with his escape. Only one likely prospect stood out, he had no choice but to chance it. With his course of action decided, he crammed needed clothing, enough food for a day or two, and his money into a briefcase. At the last minute he grabbed the photo of him with his parents taken just before the purge when they had been a happy family. Pong Ju took one last look around the apartment and walked out the door. He did not bother to lock it. It wouldn't have mattered anyway. Once his neighbors realized he was gone it would be picked clean in a matter of hours.

He took the bus across town. Had he looked through the window at the passing buildings and the homeless curled into sleeping bundles along the streets he would mourn the condition of his country thanks to the Kim regime. He had no time for mourning, nor any other emotion at the moment. Even the fear that threatened to undo him, he had to firmly reject. If he failed, he was dead. He had only the one option left. When he arrived on the south side of Pyongyang, he got off at the bus stop and continued on foot taking care to go by a circuitous route, checking for anyone that might be following. When he reached the door he sought, he was relieved to see a light still glowing through the front window curtain.

Pong Ju knocked on the door of Captain Song Jun-sang and softly called, "Please, help me in the name of my father General Pah. I am in terrible trouble."

The light in the window died and his heart sank as he was plunged into total darkness. He waited in despair. When he heard no answer from within, he turned away with no destination in mind. He heard the creak of the door behind him and his heart soared. Captain Song whispered, "Quickly, come in."

Pong Ju entered the darkened room. Again, Song whispered, "Wait here. I will relight the candle so I can see you."

When the weak light brought the man's face into view, he prayed that he was reading compassion in the man's eyes. "Keep your voice down when you answer. Now, tell me how do I know who you are? Can you prove you are General Pah's son?"

Pong Ju smiled with relief, "Yes, I have the last photo of us together taken not long before he died."

Song demanded, "Give it to me."

The captain walked over to the candle and held the photo near the light. He squinted as he studied it. "I loved your father. He was a good man and good to me. What is your name?"

"Pah Pong Ju, sir."

"So, tell me how I can help you. If I can, in honor of your father's memory, I will."

Pong Ju skirted the details and told his father's friend that he had been trying to undermine the Kim regime, but could no longer go forward as his life was in danger. He explained that he needed a passport under another name, any other documents related to permission to travel, a guide to lead him over the Yalu into China, and someone on the other side that would help him get to the airport in Dalian.

Song was silent for long moments before replying, "It won't be easy as the route you have chosen is the one most closely scrutinized by police looking for defectors, but I think I can help you. It will take several days to put everything in place and we must be more than careful in the meantime. Once we get your documents, it will be up to you. If you do anything suspicious you will be arrested and with your father's record, it is likely you would be killed. Also, do nothing that would implicate me. It was hard enough to survive the purge and I do not care to endanger my family and my own life again. If you were anyone else, I would be tempted to say no. Where are you staying now?"

"I have nowhere. I hoped you could provide shelter until we procure the documents."

"You cannot stay in my house. There's a shed on the rear of my property for gardening tools. It won't be comfortable, but as long as you don't show yourself in daylight it should be safe. It has a padlock on the door and I will take the key with me when I leave for work. I will lock you in with water, blankets, a bucket for bodily wastes, and what food I can spare. I'll let you out at night for a brief time. That's the best I can offer."

"I owe you my life and greater gratitude than I can express."

Song shrugged, "Oh well, if we cannot get those documents and get you safely on your way that may be premature."

"The important thing is that you have given me hope. Without your help I'd be a dead man."

By late afternoon of the following day, Pong Ju was miserable. He hated being cooped up, hated the reeking bucket of his own human waste. He had drunk the last of his water and was thirsty and bored. He had to remind himself that it could be a lot worse. By ten that night, it was. He had curled on his blanket and was trying to sleep when he heard the key turn in the lock and the captain's sibilant voice.

"Are you awake?"

"Yes."

"I'm sorry that I could not come sooner but after work I had to meet with someone to obtain the things you are going to need. I gave him money to pay for the documents. I hope that you can repay me as I cannot afford the expense."

"Of course, whatever you need."

"He says it will be two days before he can give me these things. You will have to endure here until then. I have more food, as much as I can spare, and fresh water. If you come out, I will show you where to empty the bucket. You have only a few minutes to stretch then you must return to the shed. I must lock you in until tomorrow night."

Before picking up the bucket, Pong Ju asked how much he owed and counted the money into Song's hand. He tucked his purse under his shirt and picked up the bucket.

"Whew. I'll be glad to dump this. I am sick of smelling it."

"I dug a hole. Put it over here and rake the dirt back over it. There is a bucket of water there to rinse it out and also wash your hands and face. That's the best I can do. Before you leave, I will bring a little hot water so you can shave. Do you have a razor and fresh clothes?"

"I do."

"Good. You must not look desperate."

"May the great Uri abogi help me."

"Yes, God help you." Song led him back to the shed and whispered good night.

Pong Ju drank some water and ate a portion of the food. Sated, he curled up on his blanket and was soon asleep. The next day passed much as the one before except that Song arrived home earlier. He cautioned that the following day he would be late as he would need to meet the man with the documents before returning. He advised Pong Ju to sleep well during the day as he would need to leave as soon as he gave him the needed papers.

Chapter 10

Quint was returning from his morning walk on the beach with Code when Buster emerged from the guest house and joined him on the walk up to the main house. It was a beautiful blue-sky morning and both men were content to enjoy the peace of the day. When they reached the veranda, they settled into deck chairs to drink the cups of coffee Teresa had just put out for them.

"You lucked up when you talked Teresa into moving here. She already knows how I like my coffee."

"You're right. Not only that, but I don't think I've ever had any better food. Mrs. Henderson was a wonderful cook, too. I still miss her as she and her husband were like surrogate parents to me." Quint looked down to hide the tears that threatened to spill from his eyes.

"Yeah, it's a damned shame Forsyth sent that asshole down here to murder them. That's hard to forget."

"That it is. Since he was looking for me, I still blame myself." Quint took a sip of coffee as he watched the waves roll to shore. Code was curled beside his chair. Unconsciously his hand dropped down to scratch Code's favorite spot behind the ears. His late parent's home by the sea had become his peaceful place. For a moment he considered selling his house in Raleigh, but he knew it was a safe bolt-hole should he ever need it. It was also closer to the University should Lila want to work there in her old job. He hoped she would. It was much safer for her than working for Gerald. Her recent accident proved that.

From inside the house he could hear Lila shouting with excitement before bursting from the door onto the veranda. "I did it! I found the bastard!"

"Are you sure?"

"Positive." Her face was beaming like a kid's at Christmas.

"Hang on. You might as well tell Gerald at the same time. Do you both have your phones?"

Lila held hers up immediately as Buster fumbled in his pocket before extracting his and holding it up as well.

"Great. I'm going to put through a conference call with Gerald. He's going to be one happy man as the President has been really leaning on him."

Lila's eyes sparkled with excitement as they waited for the call to go through. The moment they were all connected, she burst out, "I found him, Gerald."

Echoing Quint, he asked, "Are you sure?"

"Almost a hundred percent. At least I know I've found the location of the IP address. It's coming from the Baiduru Company in China."

"I've heard of them. They are doing some cutting-edge stuff with artificial intelligence, autonomous navigation, and Web management."

"Right. And that's where this gets interesting. I nosed around in their company files and using my translator program, it looks like the top dog in computer research there is a Mr. Chen Dai. Apparently, he is arrogant and a bit of a rebel, too, as there are several reprimands for insubordination in his file. If he were not really good, they would have fired him or worse long ago."

"It could be someone that works in the same department and not him. How can you be sure he's the one?"

"I can't, but my gut tells me he is. He's the best they have at this stuff. He's also been contacting someone in North Korea that seems to have vanished, as Dai's repeated attempts aren't going through."

"He's not on to you, is he?" Gerald asked.

"Not so far, and I intend to do everything I can to keep him from catching on."

"Okay, Lila…do it; and keep me posted. Quint, you ready for that fishing trip?"

"You're really serious about me going to China? I don't speak Mandarin, but Buster does. Why not send him instead of me?" Quint glanced at Buster who had a smirk on his face. Instant jealousy grabbed him. He wouldn't put it past the bastard to try to make time with Lila while he was away.

Buster's grin vanished and Quint's emerged at Gerald's next order, "You're going with him Buster. I know you speak several Chinese dialects as well as Mandarin. You will serve as translator as needed and back up muscle. Your ID will show that you are an executive assistant to Quint. I will have a replacement there tonight for you, Buster, along with both your ID's and passports. The agent will have your plane tickets as well."

"I want to go, too," Lila piped up.

"No, I need you to continue doing just what you're doing now…stay on this Dai character. I want you to track his every move."

When they hung up Lila followed Quint to the bedroom. "Dammit!" she began. Why can't I go? After all, I'm the one that found him?"

"Gerald's right, babe. He needs you here. If you were with us, we would be distracted trying to keep you safe. That could put us all in danger. You don't want that now do you?"

"No, of course not. But I worry about you. I'm counting on being the next Mrs. Cord, not the almost Mrs. Cord so you had damned well better come back in one piece."

"Don't worry. I'm aiming, too."

Quint hauled his suitcase from the closet and opened it on the bed. Code had followed them to the bedroom. He looked from one to the other and woofed. Code watched as Quint began pulling clothes from his chest of drawers. The dog left the room at a trot. Moments later he returned with his favorite toy. Dropping it by the bed, he whirled around and was gone. Returning in short order, he next dropped his food bowl by the toy. Quint and Lila were so busy packing they did not notice what he had done. The dog again darted from the room to return with his water bowl. Once more he left to come back with his leash which he dropped onto the floor with the other items. Then he gave a sharp bark.

Lila and Quint turned from the closet and looked at Code who was waiting expectantly by the bed. It was then they noticed the pile of things the dog had collected. Both began laughing.

Quint walked over and squatted beside his dog. "No, boy. I know you are tired of me leaving, but I need you to stay here and take care of Lila and Teresa. You can't go with me this time. Now go put your things back where they belong."

If a dog could cry, he would have. As it was, he hung his head and obediently began to remove the items by the bed.

Quint shook his head. "Man, that makes me feel like shit."

"Maybe I should have done that, too."

"Lila, you know I want to be with you. Maybe, when I get back, we could take a trip…as in honeymoon."

Still pouting, she murmured, "Well, maybe you should stop packing and give me a proper goodbye so I still want a honeymoon with you."

"Come here, you."

An hour later, Quint emerged from the shower and dressed. Grabbing his briefcase and luggage, he met Buster in the living room. Lila followed him out. Noting Quint's wet hair and the look on their faces, he teased. "Now, that's the kind of send-off I need. Now, if I just had a girl and a free minute…"

Lila laughed before teasing, "Hey, Buster. Is a minute all you're good for?"

Buster blushed a bright red before joining Quint and Lila in laughter. "You got me on that one, Lila."

Quint whistled for Code, who emerged from the kitchen with Teresa following. "I packed y'all a little snack. That airline food ain't worth bothering with and y'all are going to miss dinner."

"Thank you, Teresa. You're the best." Quint added, "Director Williams is sending someone to take Buster's place. You and Lila are to let either him or one of the other guards do any errands or anything else you need off property until we get back. I know that's kind of confining, but I couldn't live with myself if anything happened to y'all. Code is unhappy with me for leaving again, but maybe you can make him a special treat to cheer him up."

Code just glared. Quint added, "And then, again, maybe not. I am for sure the one in the dog house as far as my dog is concerned."

The doorbell rang, and Teresa went to answer it. Standing

aside, she waved the new man in the door. He walked into the living room and introduced himself as Kirk Young. Waving to the dining room table he asked Quint and Cord to follow him over. Lifting his briefcase onto the table, he began spreading documents across the surface.

"These are your passports, ID's, hotel reservations and tickets. You're booked from here to Charlotte tonight and then to San Francisco where you will wait for the flight to China. You'll have time on the flights to familiarize yourself with everything. Both of you have briefcases in the car with the initials of your alias on them, phones, instructions from Gerald, information on the company in China, and appropriate luggage tags."

Quint and Buster picked up the items on the table and put them in their jacket pockets.

Quint looked around the room, "Right, I guess it's time to say goodbye. I'm going to miss it here and everyone in this room. Stay safe and do what Mr. Young tells you. We'll be back as soon as we can." He then hugged Lila and told her he loved her, hugged Teresa, and then hugged Code who relented enough to nuzzle him.

Only Kirk Young would be coming back that night after driving the two men to the Wilmington airport. Lila, Teresa, and the dog stood on the front porch watching as the men drove away. It was hard to tell which of the three watching the car disappear was more downcast. Lila turned to Teresa and asked, "What say we have a drink of wine on the porch."

"That sounds, like a plan to me. I'll bring our dinner outside, too."

As they ate, their thoughts were with Quint who was on the plane to Charlotte. Both he and Buster were reading the materials in their briefcases and memorizing critical details. In Charlotte, they boarded the plane to San Francisco, delighted to see that they were in first class.

"Well, I could grow accustomed to this except for one thing. Gerald must be mighty worried about this trip to spend big bucks on these tickets. He never has before."

Quint laughed, "I suspect it was less a matter of generosity than us traveling like important businessmen."

"Yeah, that sounds a lot better than, a 'sayonara' suckers."

"It looks like Gerald has thought of everything to keep us safe. It's going to be up to us not to fuck it up."

They glanced up as the stewardess approached to ask if they would like a drink. She gave Buster an inviting smile. He was quick to order, "Make mine a whiskey sour, sweetheart."

On impulse, Quint glanced over at him before touching his sleeve. He cooed, "Make that champagne for me. We're celebrating."

Noting the arm caress, the stewardess made no comment as she turned to get the requested drinks.

Buster turned to Quint who was smirking at him, "Why in the hell did you do that? I was planning on trying to make a little time with her in San Francisco before we fly out. Now she'll think we're gay and not give me the time of day."

Buster was pissed when the woman walked back with their drinks and delivered them without that warm smile. He was still sulking when dinner and three drinks later, Quint stowed the information packet in his briefcase and reclined the seat.

"That's right, smartass. Go to sleep and let me try to repair the damage with the stewardess. She was definitely coming onto me before you screwed it up."

When they checked into the hotel at the San Francisco airport, Buster immediately buzzed off with an "I'll see you later."

"Don't miss our flight, lover boy."

"I'll be there. Right now, I need to take care of some unfinished business."

"I just bet you do. Maybe, I should have stayed awake and taken notes."

"You already have your woman. You don't need any more notes."

Quint smiled, "Damn straight."

He went up to his room and stretched out on the bed for another couple of hours sleep before he called Lila. Even with the three-hour time difference, it was too early to call. Despite having slept on the plane, he was soon sleeping again. The persistent ringing of his phone brought him to consciousness. For a moment he was disoriented as he looked around the room. Then he remembered: San Francisco.

Glancing at the phone, he saw that it was Gerald. "Hello, what have you got?"

"Lila called me a few minutes ago. Apparently, she worked all night after you left. This Chen Dai character spent hours trying to get through to North Korea before giving up. He went into total silence several hours after that. We can't tell if the Chinese are onto him, if the North Koreans are after him, or if he has done a runner."

"So, do we continue on to China or come home?"

"No, you go on like we planned. Until we know more, the Baiduru Company is still our best starting point. There is one change of plans though. The tickets to Shanghai have been changed. We're flying you to Tokyo first and from there to the base at Futenma. I want you to talk to those airmen and see what you can learn. There may be something we're missing. Once you're through on Futenma, unless we have something else on Dai, you will then go to China like we planned."

Chapter 11

Pah Pong Ju spent the next day with optimism that by nightfall he would be on his way to freedom. When he heard footsteps coming his way, he was elated. The time to go had arrived. His joy vanished as he listened to Captain Song attempting to placate someone. Pong Ju wasted no time in climbing into a trash barrel and pulling his blanket and as many grass clippings and trash as he could grab from the floor over the top of him. His heart pounded with such force, he feared whoever was with Captain Song, would hear him and discover his hiding place.

The unknown voice exclaimed, "If your neighbor is wrong and you do not have someone hidden here, Captain Song, why is there a bucket of shit in the corner? I can smell it from here."

"I am so sorry. The odor is offensive; however it is not there because I am hiding someone. You see, when I am working in the garden I often need to go. I use the bucket in here as my wife will not allow me to go outside. I come in here and use the bucket so I do not track dirt into the house. I worked late last night and because I was tired and hungry, I forgot to bury it as I usually do."

"Then you have no problem with me looking around." It was a statement and not a question.

"No, no. Please, look."

Pong Ju held his breath as the man approached the barrel and ran his hand across the grass clippings and rags that covered him.

Apparently satisfied, the man moved on. He could hear him moving tools and looking in an old trunk that was shoved against the side of the shed. After anxious minutes and allowing himself only small sips of air, he listened as their steps retreated and the door slammed shut. Again, the lock was secured. Pong Ju dared not move. He could not have said how long he huddled in cramped misery. He only knew that his legs were asleep and the rest of his body was in agony. He smelled the rank odor of adrenaline inspired by his fear. He again prayed, "Uri abogi, help me in my time of despair."

It was hours later when he heard stealthy steps approaching the shed door. A key turned in the lock, the hasp squealing lightly as it was removed. A soft creak of the hinges was followed by Captain Song's voice. "It is safe. Come out. You must leave now. It is almost midnight. You should have left an hour ago, but I was afraid to risk it. Your contact is waiting. We can only pray he will continue to wait while you try to reach him."

Captain Song watched Pong Ju emerge from the barrel. His legs collapsed beneath him when he tried to stand. The captain walked over and gave him a hand up.

"It's my feet and legs. They went to sleep." He grimaced in agony as feeling began to return.

"Give it a minute and then we go. I will take you to your contact. Put these papers in your pocket." Captain Song shook his head, "You could use a bath, shave, and change of clothes but there is no time. I will help you strap this bag of your things to your back. Perhaps, when you get across the river you can take a moment to bathe when it is safe. No matter what, you must cross the river before the night ends."

"Thank you. I know you have risked your safety and your

families for me. I will not forget and if I can ever help you I will."

"I do this in honor of your father. I need no thanks. Now, we go. Do not speak again and stay in the shadows. The night has eyes and ears."

They moved from the town into the countryside always keeping in the shadows and never speaking. A slight pressure on his elbow was all Pong Ju needed to know when to turn or stop. It was over an hour later when they came to the river. He could tell by his labored breathing that Captain Song was no longer accustomed to this much rapid walking. The captain crouched in the weeds along the river bank and hissed to Pong Ju to get down and stay hidden. Duck walking from where he left him, the captain crept along the verge of the river. Pong Ju heard the soft voice of another man informing him that the contact that was to take him across to safety had waited for them after all. Both men walked back to Pong Ju.

The captain pressed his shoulder, "I wish you good fortune. Go now."

Pong Ju whispered his thanks as the captain slipped off into the weeds and climbed the bank to the trees. He was nearly there when shots rang out and he watched his father's old friend fall to the ground. Pong Ju started to rise. He was responsible for endangering the man and wanted to see if he were dead or injured. His guide grabbed him by the arm to halt his rise.

"Don't be stupid. Leave him. You can do nothing for him now. He may just be staying down until it is safe to move. We must save ourselves. Come."

Hugging the weeds, they crawled to the river and sank into the water. Shots dug into the mud at their rear. Pong Ju quivered with fear, momentarily paralyzed by it. Again, his guide hissed in his ear to hold his breath and swim underwater. Water had always terrified Pong Ju. He was a poor swimmer, but if he wanted to live, he had no choice. He did what the man ordered, took a deep breath and began to crawl along the bottom of the river. Gradually, it deepened, and the water began to buoy him upward. He felt his lungs would burst for want of air, but he swum doggedly on for another instant before rising to the surface and gulping air. The guide rose beside him. Immediately bullets began to splat the surface of the river. They both dove again under the murky water and started swimming in the direction of the bank. Thinking he would die if he did not breathe, Pong Ju swam to the surface. His guide popped up beside him. Both sucked in air before resuming their underwater swim. Bullets continued to rake the river.

When they next came up for air, the guide stuttered breathlessly, "We are almost there. Swim towards that bunch of reeds and stay down until the North Koreans leave."

Pong Ju nodded and sank into the river to resume the swim to safety. He was almost to the safety of the shore when he felt a sharp sting on his right arm. He dared not slow to check on it with bullets still shrieking through the air. When he reached the shore, he pulled himself deep into the weeds and waited for his guide to join him. A moment later he heard a rustling in the nearby reeds and breathed a sigh of relief.

The guide whispered, "Are you all right?"

Frightened by the throbbing in his arm and the sensation of warm blood running down it, he stuttered, "I'm not sure, but I think I've been shot."

"We will stay down for a few minutes to give the guards time to move on. Then I will check it for you. In the meantime, cover the wound with your hand and press down to stop any bleeding."

It was another agonizing thirty minutes before the guide again whispered to him, "I think it is safe now to crawl on up the bank. If the shots start again, stop and find cover. Can you move?"

"I have no choice."

"Good. Let's go."

Pong Ju gritted his teeth and forced his wounded arm to help pull him through the weeds and onto the bank. No more bullets chased them. Lying still for a moment, both men paused to catch their breath."

"Now, stand up and make for those woods. We must go through them to a farm house just beyond. I want to be inside before first light. We will tend to your wound once we get there." He paused before turning back to Pong Ju, "It would help if you speak some Chinese."

"Yes, I do. I'm not fluent but I know enough to get by."

His guide just grunted acknowledgement that he had heard him, before nudging him up. Pong Ju stood and followed the man through the woods to a rough cottage standing on the edge of a field of lush turnips. Pigs were routing in a pen, and a rooster began to crow as they entered a small enclosed yard. The guide's soft knock brought an elderly man to the door. "I expected you hours ago. I heard the shots. I feared you had been killed."

The guide shook his head, "The bastards spotted us and opened fire. I'm fine, but this man has been shot in the arm and needs seeing to."

The farmer nodded to Pong Ju, "Welcome to our home. Please, come in and sit down. I'll fetch my wife to clean your wound and bandage you up. She worked as a nurse before we married so you will be in good hands."

The Guide walked to the door and turned the handle, "Good luck. I had best be going before it gets any lighter."

"Thank you for everything. I owe you my life." As Pong Ju watched him disappear into the night, he realized he had never heard the man's name. Perhaps it was preferable that way. Were Pong Ju caught he could not reveal the name of the man who had helped him cross into China.

While he waited for the farmer and his wife to return, he looked around the cozy room. He was in awe of the simple luxuries it contained...those that all but a select few enjoyed in North Korea. He could hear a soft murmur from the room the farmer had disappeared into, but the throbbing in his arm prevented him from concentrating on what they were saying. He was angry that he had been shot while grateful that his life had been spared. He could only hope that the injury would not detain him for long. He wanted to reach Incheon airport in Dalian and claim refugee status to fly to South Korea. Suddenly he wondered if he would be wiser to go to the American Consulate and tell his story. Perhaps, he would be safer in America. His musings were cut short by the farmer returning to the room followed by his wife.

While the old woman cleaned and bandaged his arm, he studied the couple. They were both old, but unlike the elderly of his own country, their flesh was ample. It was obvious to Pong Ju these farmers had much more food than his countrymen. Their clothes were also much better in quality than those of the peasants in North Korea. If poor farmers could eat and dress so well, what would the wealthier citizens in town look like?

The old woman caught his eye and smiled. "You are a very lucky young man. The bullet only passed through the outer part of your arm. If it does not become infected, you should heal quickly."

Pong Ju bowed his head. Using the polite address for the elderly, he said, "Thank you, grandmother. My name is Pah Pong Ju."

"I am Mrs. Yang. My husband is Yang Zheng. You will stay with us until my husband's friend comes for you. He will take you to Dalian as you asked."

*****

At that moment, Chen Dai, the man Pong Ju feared more than any other, was sitting in the departure lounge at Incheon waiting for a flight to Seattle. He was in even more of a rush than Pong Ju. It would not be long before the government would come looking for him. He knew too many highly technical secrets of the Baiduru Company for them to simply let him vanish. He had managed to create a fake letter from the Taiwan Office requesting his assistance on a project that had been giving them problems. He had no intentions of reporting there. He wanted to be further away and the Bellevue, Washington office was one he was familiar with. He would check into that office and make up some excuse to get into the network there. With a passport and a travel visa obtained through the Baiduru Company travel from China was expedited for him, unlike the case with most Chinese citizens. He chuckled. It was all too easy. It was too bad he would not have more time in Seattle as he liked the city, but he had no intention of staying for long at the Bellevue office. Once he had covered his tracks and erased his on-line log, he would book a ticket to Iran. Again, he chuckled. Tehran could use him, and he fully intended to use the Iranians.

Chapter 12

Buster and Quint arrived at Narita International Airport outside Tokyo under cloudy skies that burst into a deluge as the plane landed. They made their way through immigration control and to baggage claim where a crisply uniformed sergeant awaited, holding a sign above his head containing their names. Quint walked up, introduced himself and then Buster.

Reading the name tag on his chest, Quint said, "Appreciate you meeting us, Sgt. Vause. Gerald says you are taking us to Yokuta Air Base where we catch our flight to Futenma."

"Yes, sir. If you will follow me, I have a helicopter waiting. The trip by rail or car is a bit of a hassle traffic-wise, so Director Williams requested we do it this way. I guess he figured it's better than taking public transport. Considering the weather, it really is the best way. Unfortunately, it looks as though this is not going to let up anytime soon." He pointed to his left, "There is a men's room nearby if you need to go before we leave."

"I'm okay. How about you, Buster?"

"I'm cool. Let's roll."

Vause shook his head, "Looks like the bottom dropped out. We're going to get drowned on the tarmac. I don't have an umbrella. We weren't predicted to get rain until later so it didn't seem necessary."

Quint shrugged, "No problem. We won't melt, but that nice uniform is going to look the worse for wear shortly."

"Sad to say, I think you're right. Oh, well. I have another." Vause looked down ruefully. He took pride in his appearance, his tailored uniform and highly polished shoes, mostly, because he had found it attracted the attention of the few available women on base. He was tall, well formed, and with pleasing features, but the way he saw it, it didn't hurt to enhance the package. He led the two men with luggage in tow to the adjacent tarmac where a helicopter, rotor idling, was waiting. All three were drenched when they reached the helicopter. Shoes making a squishing sound, hair dripping water, they climbed aboard.

"Damn. That's a monsoon," Buster exclaimed as he settled into his seat and strapped in.

Once Quint was settled, Vause walked to the front of the helicopter and settled into the co-pilot seat. Both Quint and Buster watched the pilot as he lifted the chopper from the tarmac. Buster had been to Tokyo before, but not Quint, and he was disappointed not to get a glimpse of the city. The driving rain was so heavy they could barely see ten feet from the chopper windows, much less the ground that was quickly vanishing beneath them.

Buster glanced over at Quint who was trying to wring the water from his pants' legs. He had already removed his shoes, dumped the water on the floor and squeezed out his socks. "Sonny boy, that ain't going to make any difference. We still have to leave the chopper to catch our flight to Futenma. You heard the pilot say it's raining like hell there, too. You're just going to get soaked again."

"Hell, I know it. I was just trying to feel a little better in the meantime. Looks like we're going to look like drowned rats when we finally arrive. So much for first impressions."

"Who the hell cares?"

"Gerald told me the guy we report to, a Major John Roberts, is an arrogant asshole. I don't like to start out in an inferior position with some stuff-shirt who thinks his shit doesn't stink."

"Fuck him. All we need to do is talk to these Marston and Rawls fellows. After that we go to China, weasel our way into the Baiduru Company and start nosing around."

"Right you are. I personally don't see where the pilots in Futenma can tell us much more than what they already said in their report. If it were me calling the shots, I would have gone straight to Baiduru."

"That's the joy of government work, buddy. You go where you're told, no questions. That's why I started my own freelance business. It pays better, too. Yeah, you don't get the pension and benefits, but I make enough to handle it. I still think you should come in with me."

"Believe me. I've thought about it. I guess I feel loyalty to Gerald more than I do the CIA. As long as he's director, I'll probably stick."

"Yeah, I like Gerald, too. I've known him a long time. He's rock solid and smart as hell. He's a good man for the job. If he wasn't, I wouldn't be doing this. I can get enough work without the CIA."

For the next few minutes Quint was lost in thought. He did not hear the chatter between the pilot and co-pilot and with ground control. He thought about Lila, the events around her accident, and those in Asia. If there was some mastermind that connected them all, it was imperative they ferret him out before he could create world chaos.

It was a different kind of war. In the past it was the immediate threat of a deadly bullet or some other weapon that endangered him and others. In this war, the threat was far more insidious, unidentifiable, and remote. It became a needle in the haystack game whereby each threat had to be uncovered, chased to ground, and destroyed. It had scared the hell out of him when Forsyth's hired assassins were on his tail and shooting at him, but he had the skills to off-set that kind of threat. In this kind of war, his skills were less important than those of Lila and others who sat behind computers somewhere digging around in the ether. Theirs was an impersonal enemy, but no less deadly than an army of hostiles with bullets and bombs. He considered all of the ways that the advent of the computer, satellites, and new weaponry had changed warfare. So much of it was remote and intangible. The basic infrastructures of every country, utility, business, and person were now vulnerable to a hostile attack perpetrated by those that wormed their way through web-security protocol. All he and Buster could do was interview, interrogate, and plant seeds. Someone else would have to do the harvest.

Lost in thought, Quint had not noticed their descent until they were just before landing. He just wanted to get on the plane to Futenma and get this leg of the journey done with. However, that wasn't to be.

The pilot called back to them, "Your plane was delayed getting in because of the weather. I'm afraid you've got about an hour or so to wait. The Colonel says to get you to the officers' club and treat you to a hot meal. The chow there is pretty good."

Buster who stayed hungry wasted no time in accepting the invitation. With no real choice, Quint resigned himself to the wait. Besides it had been hours since he had eaten and he was growing hungry as well. If they ate now, perhaps they could get right into the interview with Rawls and Marston when they arrived in Futenma and then fly straight out.

Vause handed them umbrellas from a stowage locker as they hefted their luggage to leave the copter. "We're wet, but there's no sense in getting wetter. I'll get you to the officer's club, but first let's drop your bags in the office over there."

"We need them locked securely. Will that be a problem?"

"It shouldn't be. Things are pretty cramped, but there's a secure closet in the office that's not totally crammed full."

Quint raised an eyebrow, "After the bombing and fire at Futenma, were men and equipment transferred here?"

"No, we're just at capacity pretty much. None of the Futenma folks were sent here. Those that were badly burned were sent to a hospital ship for initial treatment and then those that needed more extensive medical help were flown back home. We didn't pick up any of the Futenma personnel or any equipment from there. Matter of fact, we sent them both men and equipment to get them up and running again."

"Any rumors on base as to how the bomb ended up landing on Futenma?"

"Yeah, lot's of rumors...but no answers. Most people can't believe the North Koreans are stupid enough to do something like that. Others think they're belligerent enough to do it and cunning enough to deny it was on purpose."

Quint nodded, "Yeah, it's a poser for sure?"

"Everybody figures that's why the government called in you spooks. I sure hope you find some answers as we are all wondering if we will be next." When neither man responded, he pointed to the luggage, "If you've got all your stuff. Let's go."

Vause opened his umbrella as he stepped onto the tarmac. Quint, Buster, and the pilot followed suit. With the wind hurling the rain sideways the umbrella was next to useless. Angling the umbrellas into the wind, the four men hurried towards the building at the edge of the tarmac where lights sent out a weak glow through the pelting rain. They dashed through the door, collapsing their umbrellas the minute they were in the vestibule. Quint and Buster, following the lead of the other two men, dropped their umbrellas by the door to await their next dash to the officer's club. The pilot arranged for the storage closet to be unlocked, while Quint and Buster turned their backs, removed the most critical documents, and secured them inside their shirts. They could not afford to take chances with hypersensitive information. With their luggage secured, they picked up their umbrellas and ran to a waiting van which would carry them to the club.

They were just finishing a traditional steak dinner with baked potato and salad, when Vause received a text on his phone. "Plane's here and the pilot's anxious to get underway. Seems this storm is heading towards Futenma. I suspect you guys are in for a bumpy ride."

Thirty minutes later they could confirm the prognostication. The plane was bouncing up and down like a yo-yo. Quint watched Buster growing increasingly green around the gills. Reaching over in a side pocket, he found a barf bag and offered it to him without saying a word. He himself wished he had an empty stomach as his own was beginning to feel unsettled. Taking a deep breath, he leaned back in his seat and tried to relax.

"Geez," Buster groaned, "how the hell much longer is this going to last?"

"I have no idea. The pilot said he was going to fly around the worst of it so the flight will be longer than normal."

"Good grief! You mean this is not the worst. I don't see how he is keeping the bird…"

A sudden drop that had both men worrying that the craft was not going to stabilize stole Buster's words and left him with the knuckles on both hands white as he death-gripped the seat. The plane slowly regained altitude, and Quint loosened his own grip as he swore. "Damn, Buster, I think Gerald owes us one for this. We're getting tossed around like popcorn, we're both wet as all hell, and we have to fly through the damn mother of all storms to interview two men that have already told everything they know."

"Yeah. This sucks."

If either man had been openly religious, Quint knew they would have been on their knees singing hosannas when the pilot plopped the plane onto the runway and fought the wind to get it to the base air center.

The Pilot, Ray Walker turned back to them. "Sorry about that, you guys. This has been one shitty flight. There was a time or two I thought we were going to have to bail."

Buster groaned, "Just what I need to hear. I surely don't want to be getting on another plane to go to China until this storm moves on."

"I can't say as I blame you for that. Grab those umbrellas and your stuff, and we'll get you over to the Major's office."

"What's Major Roberts like?" Quint asked.

The pilot shook his head. "That's not for me to say. You are shortly going to have the pleasure of drawing your own conclusions."

"That's what I was afraid of. Anyone that won't answer a question like that has already answered the question."

Buster laughed, but the pilot merely picked up his umbrella as he exited the plane. Buster and Quint followed him to a waiting jeep and climbed in. The driver greeted them as they thanked the pilot. Once that was done, he put the jeep in gear and tore off across the tarmac with tires squealing. Quint glanced over at Buster and shook his head. Since the plane ride didn't kill them, the kid behind the wheel seemed determine to do it. Looking back they saw a twin rooster-tail of water flying up from the rear tires.

"You in a rush to get somewhere, son?" Buster asked.

"Damn straight. Major Roberts said to haul your asses to his office the minute you land as he's tired of waiting. Sorry, but I just ain't up for another ass-chewing from the Major today."

"He sounds like a real jewel."

"Excuse me for saying anything. If he knew I told you what he said, I'd get another chewing out. Bottom line, I suspect he would be happier if he could get promoted to stateside."

Quint chuckled, "Sorry, son, I can't help you out there. And we don't plan to stick around long enough to provide anyone a character reference either. From what I hear, you're not the only one that seems less than fond of him."

Chapter 13

Lila chewed her lip as she studied her computer screen. Something was going on. She was into the computer at Baiduru that she had zeroed in on previously and was tracking, but the signature had changed. Whoever the previous user was, he was no longer at that computer. Using hacked pass codes and tracking protocol, she went after any mobile devices that might be using the signature she was after. It had been hours of frustration and she was tired. Standing up, she stretched and looked out the window at sunlight sparkling on the Atlantic. A light breeze created a few white caps beyond the breakers enticing her to take a walk to escape for a few moments before returning to the computer and beginning again. Feeling a gentle nudge against her leg she looked down. Code had his leash in his mouth and was looking up expectantly.

Lila laughed as she scratched him behind the ears, "I believe you are as ready as I am to get out of the house."

Dropping the leash at her feet, Code woofed in agreement. Lila retrieved it and snapped it into place. "Come on then. Let's see if Teresa wants to join us."

Soon the three of them, trailed by one of the security detail were walking on the edge of the breakers. Code scampered after fiddler crabs, nosed in the shallow water for treasures, and periodically shook himself…flinging water over both women. After the third such antic, Lila scolded, "No, Code. You stop that."

Code cocked his head at her and paused before taking off after another fiddler crab that was busy trying to bury itself in the concealing sand. Not to be outdone, Code scratched furiously at the vanishing crab causing it once again to scurry off with the dog snapping in its wake. A seagull landed in front of him to join the excitement until Code barked, sending the bird upward in squawking alarm.

"For a dog that grew up in Raleigh, he sure does love this beach," Teresa remarked. "At least it keeps him from missing Quint so much. When you were in the hospital and Quint was gone all those weeks, that dog moped all over the place until I took him out for a walk."

"The walk doesn't do it for me. I still miss Quint."

"I do, too. He's a good man. And you're good for him. When y'all were on the outs, he was as hang-dog as I ever saw. I couldn't get a smile out of him much less a laugh. You put the bounce back in his step when you came back."

"Thanks, Teresa," Lila looked over at the woman and grinned, "What say we go back and pour a glass of wine before dinner? Do you have time for that?"

"I've got most of dinner cooked. It sure is more work feeding these security folks as well as us, but at least they'll eat anything I put before them and ask for more."

"I can't blame them for that when I am just as bad. You're too good a cook. If I keep it up, I'll be so fat Quint won't know me when he gets back."

Teresa glanced over at Lila's slim figure. "Lila, I don't think you've got a thing to worry about. What do you say, want to go pour us a glass? I've got time for one before I serve dinner."

"That works for me. By the way, are these two security people working you too much? You know I can always help if you need me. I can't cook like you, but I can do simple stuff like chop vegetables."

"There's no need. These three don't begin to match what Buster could eat all by himself. I almost feel like I'm on holiday." Teresa laughed and shook her head with amusement. "He is worth it though. That Buster keeps me in stitches."

Lila wrinkled her nose, "Yeah, he is funny, but I can see smoke coming out of Quint's ears if I laugh too much at his jokes."

"Now, honey, that man is just jealous because he knows Buster is only half teasing when he flirts with you."

"I've wondered about ole Buster. Something tells me you're right."

"Lord, that man does like women. But I suspect he's a long way from settling down with just one."

"I didn't think Quint was ready to settle down either. He surely surprised me when he proposed."

"Judging by the way he was moping around, I wasn't too surprised. He was purely miserable when you wouldn't talk to him."

"I think we both know that last assignment with the CIA really shook him. I suspect the moping had a lot to do with that. As for this assignment, Quint is an expert at cracking codes. This is a whole new ballgame. Then he had to worry about an assassin's bullet; now who knows where, who, when, and what the threat will be. And, I seem to have lost the only thread we had on the who."

"Maybe so, but going back to what I was saying, I think it was during that time he came to realize that he wanted to marry you."

After their glass of wine on the porch, Lila returned to her computer while Teresa worked on dinner. She still could find no trace of the Chinese hacker. She tried everything she could think of but unless the jerk signed back on she was stuck. She set the computer to ping her if he popped up and went back to the kitchen to have dinner. An hour later she was back at her computer scurrying through back channels to see if she had missed a clue. It was almost bedtime when the computer pinged to let her know the guy in China was back on-line. Frantically she chased the location of the log-in before he could sign off. She sat back in her desk. Seattle! What was he doing in Seattle? Furiously she began to type locations for the Baiduru Company to see if he was traveling for business rather than doing a runner. Sure enough, the company had a location in Bellevue on the outskirts of the city. That explained the new location, but it still left her puzzled that the protocol at the former location in China had changed.

Lila picked up her phone and called Gerald Williams to let him know the hacker was now in Seattle, presumably at the Baiduru office in Bellevue. After she hung up, Gerald fiddled with his pencil until it snapped. He tossed it into the waste basket. His secretary once asked him why he used so many pencils. He was embarrassed to tell her that a pencil was frequently the focus of his frustration. He wondered just how many he had broken over the years in the CIA. Once again, he was unsure of what to do. Should he have Quint and Buster go to China as planned, or should he reroute them to Seattle after they left Futenma? He put his feet on his desk, leaned back and closed his eyes. The soft hum of voices from the outer office was lulling. Ten minutes later he put his feet on the floor, sat up and reached for his phone. He would have Lila continue tracking to see if the man was staying in Seattle more than a few days or if he popped up somewhere else. Until he knew more, he decided to go forward with his initial plan. Even if this character was in Seattle on a short business trip, Quint and Buster could still introduce themselves at Baiduru and initiate the first steps to getting to the hacker when he returned.

It was also essential to surmise whether or not the Chinese company was behind the hacks or if the man was acting alone. It didn't make sense to him that the company would risk an international business empire by zeroing in on governmental targets in North Korea and Japan, and then implicating an American plane in a supposed attack. He still thought it far more likely that the hacker was some deranged lone wolf. What his motivation was, Gerald could only guess and none of the guesses looked that good. If he had done a runner, that was another issue. That could also be corroborated with Baiduru. At some point he might well have to put his cards on the table and tell Baiduru his suspicions about their employee. He suspected they would sing like canaries if they thought the CIA was after them.

*****

Chen Dai was tired after the long flight, he would go to the hotel and tomorrow buy needed time by reporting to the local company office. He could make up some reason for his visit to the local office, and perhaps call the office in China to report on a problem or status, thus keeping the Baiduru Company ignorant of his use of their technology to cover his track and plan his next steps. It would take time to establish a contact in Iran and an invitation to work there. Until he had achieved that, he would be shut down unless he kept Baiduru on the string. He copied down some company contacts prior to leaving, but had never personally interacted with them. With his decision made, he picked up his bag and walked to the taxi line. After a five-minute wait, he was in a cab bound for the Hotel Regency Seattle which was only minutes from the Baiduru office located in a sleek high-rise office building in downtown Bellevue. The company had an account at the Regency so he would have no problem getting a room at company expense. He did not know how long it would be before he had a paying job in Iran, and he could not afford to burn through his own funds.

Dai settled back into his seat and resigned himself to the rush hour traffic. Soon he would be at the hotel. The thought brought a smile to his face. The last time he stayed, one of the girls at reception…a beautiful Asian named Feng Li …had made his welcome a very warm one. He had fantasized many times of the nights they had enjoyed one another in his suite. He had not kept in touch, so he did not know if she was still employed at the hotel.

Dai paid the taxi, signaled the bellman to take his bags and walked into the hotel lobby. He paused to admire the sweeping wooden staircases that soared into the huge atrium-like space. Potted plants and sparse modern furniture gave it an Asian aesthetic that appealed to him. He stood for a moment in silent appreciation. China had come a long way since the various disastrous programs, but the United States was still far above what was available to him there. Certainly, his modest apartment in China looked seedy in comparison to this elegant space. He walked over to the reception desk where the three men and a woman were helping other clients register. He focused his attention on the woman. Recognizing her when she glanced up to signal the next hotel guest to register, Dai smiled and walked over to her line. He could tell by the momentary pause in what she was doing that she recognized him as well. The man ahead of him was slow and fumbling, taking forever to produce a credit card and reservation confirmation number. Dai could only hope the hotel was not fully booked as he did not have the money to stay in another of anywhere near the same quality. Finally, the elderly man stumbled away from Feng Li with plastic access key card in hand.

Dai took his place in front of Li, and smiled. "Li, what a joy to see you again after so long away.

"Ah, Dai, you have come back. Do you have a reservation?"

He could tell by the cool tone of her voice that she was unhappy that he had never bothered to get in touch with her during the months since his last trip. "You must forgive me for not contacting you, Li. I have been very busy with my work, but that is no excuse for ignoring a beautiful woman who gave me the most pleasant moments of my life."

Her voice was a little softer when she repeated her question, "So, Dai, have you a reservation with us?"

"The request from the local office was last minute, thus I left it to my secretary to arrange the reservation as I barely had time to pack. She is very efficient. I am sure I must have one." He chuckled inwardly at the idea of the company giving him a secretary.

"Give me a moment, and I'll see what she reserved for you." Li busied herself at the computer for several minutes. Finally, she looked up, "I can't seem to find a reservation. Let me see what I can do. The hotel is totally booked, but there may have been a cancellation."

"Please, that would be great. I will be having a serious talk with my secretary when I return." As Li continued to search for availability, Dai added, "I hope you will forgive me and allow me to take you to dinner tonight?"

"I'm working tonight."

"Tomorrow night?"

"If you promise not to be so negligent in future, maybe." She did not look up when she said it, but he could hear the smile in her voice. After another minute of searching, she announced, "You're in luck. We had a cancellation of one of our nicest suites a moment ago. I think you will enjoy it. This one comes with a lovely Jacuzzi bath, and I will give it to you at the rate for a regular room. Baiduru does enough business with us that should be no problem."

"I hope I will not have to enjoy the Jacuzzi alone?"

"Hmm, dinner first and then we'll see." She flashed him a smile full of promise as she handed him the envelope with the ubiquitous plastic coded electronic pass key.

Dai accepted it with a grin and a wink, "Tomorrow night it is."

He was still smiling when he walked into the luxurious suite. Walking over to the window, he opened the curtain and looked out at the distant expanse of water. He was tired and secretly glad that Li was unavailable for the night. He decided to order a room service dinner and then after triggering another little pre-selected surprise, he would go to bed. He needed to be fresh tomorrow when he arrived at the company office, and he wanted time to fine tune his excuse for being there. He did not need any difficulty arising from calls about his arrival going back to the home office.

Chapter 14

Quint returned his phone to his pocket and turned to Buster, "That was Gerald. It seems our character has cut out for Seattle. He still wants us to go to China to see what we can learn there. If it looks as though his trip to Seattle is on the up and up, we are to wait until this guy returns and try to make contact. If it looks fishy, we'll see what we can learn from the Baiduru Company. If he leaves Seattle, hopefully Lila will be able to track him for us."

"I have a feeling my ass is going to be tired of plane seats before this is over. Geez, I didn't bring enough underwear for a long trip."

"Neither did I. Looks like we have two options: in room laundry or a shopping trip if and when we get to Seattle."

"Yeah, looks like."

"Let's check in with this major Roberts, and then we'll go talk to the fly-boys and see what they can tell us about the Osprey crash. Gerald didn't say anything about the bomb that took out most of the base. I suppose he is handling that through another channel."

"Probably wouldn't hurt to ask around about that either, maybe they learned something through the grapevine here that didn't make it to Washington."

"Not a bad idea," Quint agreed.

They walked in the direction indicated by the driver who

declined to escort them, noting the vast destruction to the base as they did so. Only the buildings on this side of the base appeared to have survived relatively intact; many of the others were heavily damaged or blackened shells. The odor of burned wood, rubber, and human bodies still lingered in the damp atmosphere. Both of them were glad to reach the air-conditioned office and take a deep breath of less fetid air.

With Buster on his heels, Quint walked up to the corporal manning the desk in the outer office. "We're here to see Major Roberts. CIA Director Gerald Williams arranged for us to see him before we interview the two pilots of the downed Osprey."

"Yes, sir, Major Roberts is expecting you. I'll just let him know you're here. You may take a seat over there if you'd like." He pointed to two straight-backed wooden chairs that were against the far wall.

Buster eyed the uncomfortable looking chairs and shrugged, "My butt is pretty tired of sitting right now. I think I'll stand."

Quint did not move to a chair either, but remained staring expectantly at the corporal. "We don't plan to be kept waiting. After all, I hear it's dinner hour for the Major."

"Yes sir. I'll let him know you're here."

In seconds the corporal was back in the reception area beckoning them to go into the Major's office. Quint looked over at Buster and lifted an eyebrow, before both men walked into the inner office. Just inside the door, Quint paused and looked around at the relative luxury of the office: cushy leather chairs, an oriental carpet, and elegant desk lamp. He took his time letting his eyes settle on the major. He figured he could play the intimidation game, too.

Major Roberts indicated the two chairs in front of his desk, but neither Quint nor Buster acknowledged the invitation to sit. Quint watched the Major's mouth quirk to one side in irritation before he spat, "It's about time you got here. You were expected hours ago."

"If you had arranged better flying weather, perhaps we would have been on time." Quint gave him a hard eye, "Major, we are not here to inconvenience you or discuss the weather. We were ordered to see you first as a mere courtesy. Our sole reason for coming is to interview the two Osprey pilots that ditched their bird to keep from hitting a Chinese chopper. As soon as we do that, we'll be on our way. If you will tell us where we can find them that should conclude our business with you."

Roberts bristled as he demanded, "Who in the hell do you think you are? Are you aware of my position here and the influence I have in Washington?"

"With all due respect, sir, assessing your influence and position are not part of our job description." Quint kept his voice flat, his eyes never leaving the major's.

Breaking eye contact, Roberts looked down at his desk and shuffled several papers around. Both Quint and Buster knew he was stalling. Finally, he looked up and said, "Corporal Duncan will take you to Marston and Rawls. They are expecting you. I believe that is all, gentlemen. Please feel free to leave."

"A pleasure, sir." There was no mistaking the contempt in Quint's brisk nod to the man.

When they cleared the office, Buster glanced back over his shoulder, and muttered, "Yeah, a real pleasure to leave. What an arrogant asshole." He grinned at Quint, "I don't think he liked you much.

"A mutual sentiment: I couldn't stand the bastard." Quint

shrugged as though to throw off the meeting with Roberts. "Let's find the fly-boys and then get the hell out of here. I'm beginning to hate this whole damn trip."

"That works for me, pal."

The corporal chuckled but said nothing as he led them from the office building. After another three hundred feet they arrived at a low squat structure on the edge of the damaged airstrip. Pointing to it, he informed them, "That was one of the flight offices. It's not of much use with most of the planes evacuated, but Major Roberts is not too happy with the gentlemen you're about to meet so I guess he didn't feel like offering a nicer location. He's got them pretty much tied down since the plane crashed. They weren't real fond of Major Roberts before the incident and are less so now. The fact they don't seem to mind showing it just pisses off the Major even more. The rumor is they have asked for a reassignment."

Buster laughed, "I like them already."

Duncan grinned, "Yeah, so do I. I requested another assignment, too."

Quint smiled, "Good luck, Corporal. I hope it comes through soon."

Duncan opened the office door and stepped aside for Quint and Buster to enter. The two men they were seeking were at a folding table playing a game of poker, several empty beer bottles sat on the floor around their chairs. Rawls waved the men aside, muttering, "Give me a minute. I'm not about to let Marston beat me, when I know he can't play worth a damn."

Both men drew another card and placed the new card in their hands with the two they already held. Rawls frowned as he shuffled his cards around.

"Hey, Rawls, you taught me all you know. Take pride that I finally caught on," Marston laughed as he slapped an ace on top of the two that were already turned up. "You lose. Now hand over that pack of gum and be glad we aren't playing with money."

Rawls took a package of gum from his pocket and slapped it down on the table. Marston picked it up, peeled back the wrapper and offered it to the others. When all had declined, he put the gum on the table, stood up, and extended his hand. Before he could introduce himself, the building swayed as a sudden blast ripped the air. Dust sifted down from overhead covering them in a grey cloud that settled onto every surface in the room. Coughing they ran to the door and burst outside gasping for air.

Buster looked at the others, "What the hell was that?"

"Crap. It appears we've been bombed again." Marston pointed in the distance where an orange glow was beginning to light up the sky. "At least it landed in the same spot as the last one. A few hundred yards more and we'd have been history."

Rawls chuckled as he looked back at the main office building. "What luck, it looks like it missed Roberts again, too."

Sirens blared in the distance as fire trucks raced towards the burning area. Neither Marston nor Rawls made a move to leave to assist the bombed area, but stood with Quint and Buster as they gazed at the breaking pandemonium. Quint glanced at the two men they had come to interview, "Do you guys need to skip this to help out over there? If you think you should go, please do. This will keep until you see if you're needed."

"According to Major Roberts, we are to stay out of the way. Seems we are on restriction until he decides to play nice. So, fuck him, let's get on with it. Besides, there are no people in that area anymore and most of the buildings were already useless shells.

About all that can be done is to put out the fire so it doesn't spread over here. The fire brigade will see to that."

The four men trooped back into the squalid little building and seated themselves as best they could. Quint dug around for his notepad and a pen as the two pilots shifted in their seats, both wondering what more they could add to the statements they had already given in Shanghai and again in Futenma.

Quint looked up from his note pad and read the first question he had jotted down. "Did either of you notice anything out of the ordinary with your Osprey's operating system prior to the time you lost control of the bird?'

Marston answered while Rawls merely shook his head, "No. Everything was cool. It was a routine training mission and we were on the prescribed path as you can see in our log."

"When did you first see you had a problem?"

Marston paused, closed his eyes, and pictured himself back in the bird. "Everything was fine, like I said, when the bird just suddenly stopped responding. We were flying at a little higher altitude and on a different track than the approaching Chinese helicopter which should have passed uneventfully. Without any warning, we dropped to the same altitude as the helicopter and were on a direct path to crash into it. I tried repeatedly to get the controls to respond and nothing I did worked. At that point, I knew the only way to avoid a crash and some serious problems with the Chinese was cut power and go into the sea."

"I see. Sargeant Rawls, what were you doing while this was happening?"

Rawls glanced over at Marston, "I was busy trying to determine what was going on with the instrument panel. Everything looked normal. There were no warning lights, nothing to give us a clue. When Marston said he was going to crash it, I sent out a May-Day. We had just flown over one of our ships. With the floating time we had, we figured they could reach us before the bird sank. As luck would have it, a damned Chinese patrol got to us first."

Buster looked at Quint and shrugged before turning to Marston. "What happened then?"

"They picked us up, took us to shore, and then we were taken to Shanghai for some serious questioning before our folks there could get us cleared to return to Futenma. When we got here, we were grilled again by Major Roberts."

Quint asked, "Since you gave your statements can either of you think of anything that you might have failed to mention?"

"We have racked our brains. It is the weirdest damn thing. What is so frustrating is after they picked up the bird and brought it back here, every instrument on it was perfect. The Major wants to act like we were jerking off and the crash is our fault. We didn't either one take too kindly to the insult, and were a bit less than respectful, you might say."

Quint and Buster grinned at one another. Shuffling his papers, Quint extracted another sheet. "Is there anything you can tell us about the first bombing that you noticed?"

"We were in our bunks. It was night and since we were on restriction, we were pretty much ready to go to sleep. That's when we heard the bomb. We went out to try to help, since it was chaos and there were a lot of badly burned men. We did what we could to help those that were not past the point of no return. One of them was groaning pretty badly, so I went to him and gave him a drink of water. Just before he died, he told me that the radar system had blacked out. He never saw the bomb coming."

Buster nodded at the two men, "How much longer you got in?"

"We're both up for renewal, but I'm bailing."

Rawls nodded, "I've had enough, too."

"I run a little operation doing jobs for the government… contract work. I could use a couple of good pilots if you're interested."

"That works for me. How about you, Rawls?" Marston glanced at this buddy.

"Sure. If the pay is good and the work is interesting. It's got to beat the hell out of dealing with that asshole."

Buster laughed, "Believe me, it will beat the hell out of that."

Quint looked at the two men and smiled, "Buster's a good man and a good employer. The pay is a lot better than what you're doing now, too."

"That's right, and you will no longer have to deal with the Roberts types. I'll give you my contact info and as soon as you are mustered out, call me."

"Will do."

Quint nodded, "Now let's see if we can get a flight out of here to take us to China."

Marston looked in the direction of an unharmed hangar. He then turned and pointed in the direction of the blaze. He remarked. "Shouldn't be a problem. This bomb just finished taking out what the first bomb left over there. The birds that weren't damaged in the first bomb are all in the other direction. We would be happy to fly you out, but there's no chance Roberts would allow that."

Buster handed the two men his business card, and they all four shook hands. He and Quint walked back to the main office satisfied that the trip had provided no new information. They were both relieved that the second bomb had missed them as well as the still functioning part of the base. Quint hoped it was just a coincidence that they happened to be there when the second hit occurred. Otherwise, it was possible the hacker was onto them…but as to how, he had no clue.

When they approached the hangar, and ignoring the rain that continued to pelt them, Quint stopped and stared at it for a moment. "I want to talk to the radio guys and see if anyone picked up on the latest incoming missile before we leave."

They entered the office where the radar operator was steadily swearing. He looked up as they walked in before immediately returning to the radar screen. Typing furiously at his computer, he continued to swear.

Quint introduced Buster and himself before asking, "Hey man, did you have any warning there was an incoming?"

"No, sir. It's freaking me out. It's just like last time. I was tracking the missile, and it seemed to be on the normal test trajectory until it suddenly veered towards us. It was too late to do more than holler before it hit us. My screen was acting funny, too. I only just now got the son-of-a-bitch back up." He didn't have time to say anymore when the shrill buzzing of his phone cut him off. "Fuck! Roberts is going to chew my ass out again. He acts like I dropped the damned thing. What the hell does he think I could do when we had only seconds of warning."

"We feel for you, buddy."

Their pilot was standing in the background shaking his head. None of them envied the radar operator. He nodded to Quint and Buster, "You guys ready to go to China?"

Chapter 15

Pong Ju was sitting in the holding area of the airport in Dalian. He rubbed his arm periodically but it did nothing to alleviate the persistent throbbing of his wound. He could not help fidgeting in his hard-plastic seat. It had already been two hours and they still had not called him into the office for interrogation. The murmur of the television on the wall across from him caught his attention when the program was interrupted for a special report. Pong Ju stared in shock at the screen. The minute he saw the U.S. base in Futenma had been struck by another missile, he knew Dai was responsible. The man still had the coordinates from the initial attack, so a repetition was easy to accomplish even without Pong Ju's help. Pong Ju was so entranced by the telecast that he did not hear his name called. It was only when the assistant came and tapped him on the shoulder that he turned from the television screen. In a daze, he followed her into the inner office.

He took the chair she indicated and bit his lip in nervous anticipation of the questioning that he must successfully endure in order to be allowed to seek refuge in South Korea. The Chinese official facing him looked bored at dealing with yet another refugee from North Korea. Pong Ju shifted in his seat as the man pored over the paperwork he had filled out prior to being told to wait in the outer office. Every time the man's eyebrows raised, Pong Ju held his breath. When he had finished with the papers, he laid them on his desk and lifted a grim visage. Pong Ju's heart sank. He was going to be returned to North Korea where he would be sent to a labor camp to die slowly or shot before a firing squad like his father. It was time to play the only card he had left.

"I have information about the North Korean attacks on Japan and the U.S. base on Futenma. I ask that you allow me to speak to the American Embassy and request refugee status to the United States."

"Then why did you fill out these papers asking to be allowed to enter South Korea? You're wasting my time here."

"I'm sorry, sir. I was unsure what to do as the information I have affects a lot of countries."

"Hmm." Pong Ju held his breath while the man mutely stared at him. After several long minutes, he said, "Go back to the reception area and wait there. I need to make some calls."

"Yes, sir. Thank you, sir. Please help me. My life is in danger." Pong Ju bowed as he backed out of the room. He could only hope that his obsequiousness pleased the bureaucrat that held his life in his hands.

Pong Ju sat in the same hard plastic chair for another two hours. His half-hearted attempt to watch the news was interrupted when a tall westerner walked into the reception area, glanced around, and started his way. Pong Ju stood up and bowed as he waited for the man to come nearer. He hated the acrid odor of adrenaline induced sweat that announced his anxiety to any who came near. The man studied him for a moment causing Pong Ju to tremble with fear.

"You are Pah Pong Ju?" His voice was deep, his face grim, as he asked the question in heavily accented Korean. Despite the accent, Compton had a very good grasp of the Korean vocabulary and grammar. Pong Ju was grateful that he did not have to respond in English as he had little command of Compton's native language.

Pong Ju gave a quick nod of his head. Keeping his head bowed, he struggled to calm himself. His answers to this man's question were vital to his survival. He did not know how much he dared reveal of his own culpability. He could only pray that he could implicate Chen Dai without creating even larger problems for himself. Yet, he had information that the U.S. must want. If he told them who was behind recent attacks on their base on Futenma, as well as the near collision with the Chinese helicopter that had created a crisis with both China and North Korea, surely they would be grateful enough to grant him asylum.

"Mr. Pah, my name is Donald Compton. I am with the CIA. Do you know what that is?"

Pong Ju gave another quick nod of his head.

"Mr. Pah. I don't bite so it is okay to talk to me. In fact, you're going to have to talk to me if you want my help getting you out of here. Do you understand?"

Pong Ju straightened up. Just in time he caught himself and instead of nodding, he replied. "Thank You."

"I am taking you into my custody. We're going to my office where you are going to answer some very hard questions. If you are not totally honest with me, you're going back to North Korea. Is that clear?"

"Yes, sir. I understand."

"Good let's go before the Chinese change their minds about releasing you to me."

Pong Ju followed the American to a Ford car that was waiting at the curbing. He unlocked the car and motioned Pong Ju to take the front passenger seat. Compton removed the diplomatic sticker from the windshield once he was settled behind the wheel. Pong Ju admired the car with quiet satisfaction. He had never been in a private car before. Not even his father had owned a car, and he had been one of the more prosperous North Koreans. Pong Ju rubbed his seat enjoying the tactile sensation of the leather. Compton glanced at him as he reached over and turned knobs on the dash. Pong Ju jumped when music began to play. It seemed to come at him from all sides. He looked at Compton with a question in his eyes.

"It's called surround-sound…stereo. Have you ever been in a car before Mr. Pah?"

"No. Few of my countrymen have cars."

"Well, if you manage to get to the States, you're going to see more cars than you ever dreamed of. Just about everyone there has a car. In fact, there are too damned many cars jamming the roads."

"I never dreamed of being able to go to the U.S., but now I think it is the only place that I can be safe. If I am sent back to North Korea, they will kill me like they killed my father. Please help me."

"That's going to depend on you, Mr. Pah. Certainly, I cannot blame you for not wanting to go back. However, you have to provide answers to some very serious questions. We cannot allow just anyone into our country." Compton paused, "I don't suppose you speak English?"

"Only a little that I learned for my job."

Compton glanced over at Pong Ju before concentrating on the traffic leaving the airport. For the next thirty minutes, he said nothing. Pong Ju was content to observe the driving process and the passing scenery. He noted that China was far more progressive than his own country. Its streets were crowded with bicycles, motor scooters, buses, and cars. There were people bustling along the sidewalks carrying bulging shopping bags. He could not help but contrast the scene with the streets in his own country.

He rubbed his wound again but the pain seemed to be getting worse. He hesitated to ask for a doctor, but his arm was getting no better and it felt feverish to him. Compton glanced over at him as he rubbed his arm.

"I see your arm is bandaged. Is it giving you trouble?"

"I was shot crossing into China. The farmer who took me in had his wife clean and dress it, but it is getting more painful. I think I should have a doctor look at it."

"We have one on call. I'll see that he checks it out. We don't have much further to go and it's late, so any interview can wait until tomorrow. The doctor can see you tonight. He will give you something for pain and check for infection. You will be locked in as that is safer for you and since I'm responsible, safer for me. There is nowhere you can go in China now, so don't think about trying to escape. Our security detail is armed, too, so unless you want another bullet hole in you just be grateful, we agreed to take you. You are going to have to stay put until we decide what is best. I hope your information is worth all the trouble you are causing."

"Don't worry. I will not try to leave. I want your help to get to the U.S. If you don't want me there, please send me to South Korea. I cannot go home. I know too much and I..." Pong Ju choked back a sudden need to confess his complicity in Chen

Dai's attacks.

When they arrived at the consulate, Compton checked in and arranged for a doctor. Next, Pong Ju was shown to the room that he would occupy until determination was made as to what to do with him. Pong Ju nearly laughed when the agent apologized for what he called sparse accommodations. For Pong Ju, it was the nicest room he had ever had. The bed had a thick mattress with a down duvet and large fluffy pillows. There was a sitting area with two comfortable chairs, a television on the wall, and a mini fridge where Compton pointed out drinks and snacks. An adjoining bathroom was furnished with plush towels and toiletries. Pong Ju grinned with delight as Compton left, saying he would see him in the morning.

Pong Ju was playing with the remote when a soft knock on the door was followed by a key turning in the lock. He looked up as a middle-aged Chinese man walked into the room with a black bag in his right hand. The doctor greeted him in Korean and asked him to sit in the chair nearest the lamp. When he was seated, the Doctor who introduced himself as Zhou Bao Ping, unwrapped the bandage on his arm and began prodding the wound. He could not help wincing at the sharp pain. Dr. Zhou's face was grim as he muttered to himself.

Straightening up the doctor said, "Your arm is badly infected. Without careful treatment, you could lose it. I am going to disinfect the wound then I will give you a shot of antibiotic and some pain pills for tonight. First I will inject painkiller into your arm as this is going to be painful."

Pong Ju nodded in understanding as he watched the doctor arrang the things in his bag on a clean cloth which he had spread on the table beside the chair. The sudden sting of the needle caused him to grimace. Soon his arm felt numb. As the doctor began to debride the wound, he fastened his attention on the far wall and gritted his teeth. Even with the painkiller, it still hurt. It was not long before he felt his arm being wrapped with gauze, and he looked down to see what the doctor was doing.

"I'm going to give you a shot of antibiotic now and a supply of pills. I need you to take four a day, four hours apart beginning in the morning. You have enough to last five days. I will check on you daily until I see that you are healing properly. This bandage will be changed each day until any drainage stops. If you wish to bathe, do not wet this arm. Understand?"

"Yes. And thank you, Dr. Zhou."

"You are welcome." Zhou smiled, "That arm is going to feel a lot better. Now go to bed and sleep. I will see you sometime tomorrow."

Careful not to wet his arm, Pong ju cleaned as best he could, brushed his teeth with the articles left in the bathroom, and crawled into bed wearing his only clean pair of underwear. The things he had worn for the last two days were hand-washed and hanging across the shower bar to dry. By the time his head touched the pillow, he was falling asleep.

It was not until he heard a knock on his door that he awakened and lifted his head. Again, he heard the lock turn, and this time a young woman entered carrying a tray. In rapid Chinese she began talking as she pointed at the various items on the tray. He understood little of what she was telling him. Hugging the sheet to his bare chest, he waited for her to leave before he moved to the table and looked at his breakfast. It was the most food he had ever had at one time. He stared in amazement at the basket of three rolls with jam and butter, the slices of bacon and links of sausage, the scrambled eggs, juice, and carafe of coffee. He was suddenly ravenous as had eaten almost nothing for days. As he was finishing breakfast, he remembered the pills and took one with the last of his coffee. He looked sadly at the rolls he had been too full to eat. Not wanting to waste them, he carefully wrapped them in a napkin and put them in the bag holding the meager possessions that he carried when he fled. Constantly faced with the real threat of starvation, he, like other North Koreans, had learned to treasure food and waste nothing.

Pong Ju was dressed and waiting quietly when Compton's voice followed a knock on the door. Pong Ju rose when he entered doing his best to keep from shaking. If Compton had come to take him for questioning, the next few hours were the most important of his life as they would decide whether he would live in freedom or be returned to North Korea to die. "Are you ready for me to be questioned, Mr. Compton?"

"I would like to get on with it as it doesn't feel right to keep you under lock and key, however Washington wants you kept locked in here until they send someone to conduct the interview. At least it looks like you will get a chance to let that arm heal and watch all of the television you want. By the way, the doctor will be in shortly to change your bandage. After that, if you would like, I can have someone escort you to the courtyard for an hour or so outside in some fresh air?"

"Thank you, I would like that." Pong Ju frowned, "Do you think it will be long before this man comes from Washington?"

"It shouldn't be more than a couple of days. He had to go to China first to visit a Chinese company and then he will fly here."

Pong Ju felt the blood drain from his face and bowed his head to keep Compton from seeing how shaken he was. Surely, the government in Washington was not already after Dai. The man was so careful to cover his tracks and so clever that he would never unknowingly expose himself. If they already knew about Dai, what information could he use to buy his own freedom? Would both he and Dai be punished for their part in the series of 'accidents?' Did he dare even mention Dai? He considered using the animosity of the current regime and the murder of his father as sufficient reason to plead for political asylum. It was critical to consider the full ramifications of anything he said and what should be withheld during the time he waited to be interviewed.

Compton stared at the top of Pong Ju's bowed head and waited for him to say something more. When he didn't, he asked, "Is something bothering you that you want to talk about? Perhaps, I could help you."

"Oh, no, everything is fine. I think I am still a little groggy from the medication and not thinking clearly." Pong Ju paused, "I think I should begin learning English while you hold me here. Do you have books that I could use to help me?"

"If we don't have any in house, I'm sure I can round up one. I'll also look for a Korean/English dictionary."

"Thank you. You are very good."

"No problem. I need to run as I have a number of things to do. I'll have someone get the books to you by afternoon."

Pong Ju bowed as Compton left him. He barely registered the key turning in the lock. Walking to the bathroom, he washed his face and cupped his hands for a large gulp of water. Breathing deeply, he returned to the chair by the television and sat lost in brooding thought. Where was Dai and what was he up to? Was he trying to find him? Or even more chilling, was Chen Dai trying to pin all of the blame for the incidents on him. China was big, but there were only so many places where North Koreans tried to enter, and as a Chinese, Dai would know them all and could have alerted the authorities to have him arrested.

Chapter 16

The taxi from the airport in Beijing took Quint and Buster down 10th Street into the Haidian District to the modern steel and glass structure, home to Baiduru...an international company with the second largest search engine in the world. Founded by Chong Lai, a graduate of nearby Peking University who had worked for a time at a New York company that was a division of Dow Jones, the Baiduru company had made him one of the richest men in the world with a net worth of over fifteen billion. They entered the pristinely beautiful building and were escorted to the reception area of Chong's office. Gerald Williams had already scheduled the appointment and given Quint permission to divulge what the CIA believed a Baiduru employee had been doing surreptitiously.

Chong rose from his desk when Quint and Buster entered and walked around it to greet them. After the three had shaken hands and introduced themselves, he gestured to the two Americans to be seated in comfortable leather chairs across from his desk. As Chong Lai returned to his desk, Quint took the opportunity to study him. His was a youthful fifty years of age with a slim physique and a pleasant, open smile. His mannerisms were westernized and friendly.

After Lai was seated, Quint began, "Thank you for seeing us, Mr. Chong. After the phone call from the Director of the CIA, I am sure this is an unpleasant occasion for you."

Lai laughed; when he spoke, his English was flawless, "That is an understatement. I have prided myself on this company and what we have achieved. It makes me furious that an employee would use our resources to cause harm. Mr. Williams did not tell me a great deal on the phone, but indicated you would give me greater detail. As you can imagine, I am beyond eager to learn what you have discovered. However, before we do that, I have arranged tea to be served."

Buster sighed with relief that he would not need to use his rusty Mandarin as Chong Lai's English was fluent. Leaning back in his chair, he waited for the tea, taking the opportunity to study the office. On his desk, Lai had a photo of his wife whom he met while both were studying in the States. Beside her picture was another of his two daughters and son.

Noting the direction of Buster's gaze, Lai said, "The photos you see are my family. Have you any children?'

Buster smiled, "If I do, I have not been informed. You see, neither Quint nor I are married."

"Ah, a good answer." Lai chuckled. He had a natural charisma that instantly put his visitors at ease.

Once their tea was served, Quint remarked, "Baiduru, I heard that means 'many times.' I believe you took the name from a poem?"

"Yes, one of my favorites called 'Green Jade Lantern Festival.' Do you know it, Mr. Cord?"

"I'm sorry I don't. And, please call me Quint. My cohort goes by Buster."

"With pleasure and you must call me Robby, my Americanized name." Leaning forward in his chair, Lai's face became somber. He focused intently on Quint as he said, "So, tell me, what have you learned about this employee you suspect of sabotaging vessels."

Quint began by describing Lila's initial tracking of the man and her accident immediately after she succeeded in locating him. He then listed the crash of the ferry in North Korea, the destruction of the Japanese fishing village, the near crash of the US osprey with a Chinese helicopter, and the two attacks on Futenma...all the result of unexplained malfunctions of operating systems. He explained Lila's continued tracking of the hacker that she identified as possibly being Chen Dai, an employee of Baiduru. He also mentioned a possible accomplice in North Korea that seemed to have disappeared. He did not add that the accomplice might be in CIA custody in Dalian, as the likelihood of that was a bit far-fetched. He did not tell Lai that Lila had tracked the man to Seattle as he wanted to see if Baiduru had sent him there or if Chen Dai was on the run.

Lai rose from his chair and asked to be excused for a moment. He left the office and was back moments later. "I have requested this man's personnel file and current assignments. In time, we should also be able to track any unauthorized contacts with North Korea. I expect to have much of the information in a matter of minutes. Once I have looked it over, I have requested that Mr. Chen report to this office for questioning. We should have this matter resolved very quickly and if Mr. Chen is the culprit, he will be turned over to the authorities for punishment. The Osprey incident created some negative press and difficulties between China and the US. I look forward to putting that behind both your country and mine. I want to say how much I appreciate being informed of this by your government and the courtesy you do me by accepting my innocence in any of these events that you think Mr. Chen instigated."

"None of us ever believed you would risk your company by doing something like this. It didn't make sense. You have far too much to lose and have no enmity with the U.S."

For the next thirty minutes, Lai grilled the two men on the details of the various incidents and how Lila was able to tie Chen to them. He was fascinated as Quint detailed Lila's expertise in tracking cyber hackers to Chen.

"I would like to hire this woman. We could use someone with her skills."

"I don't believe I can allow that, Robby." Quint smiled at Lai's raised eyebrows. "You see, we are engaged to be married. I don't want my wife living so far away. Also, I think our CIA director would be very unwilling to let her go."

"I can well understand. Such expertise is beyond valuable."

A knock on the door stopped conversation as Lai buzzed the person in. A secretary walked over and handed him a sheaf of papers.

Lai spoke to her in English, "Thank you. Did you notify Chen Dai that I want him in my office in fifteen minutes?" Neither Quint nor Buster reacted to what they knew to be a futile request for the man to report.

In equally fluent English, she responded, "I tried, sir. Unfortunately, Mr. Chen is not in the office here. His office director said he is in Taipei. I checked that office, but they said he isn't there, and they never requested that he come. In those papers I provided you have the email they supposedly sent Mr. Chen requesting his help, as well as his response. I also ran a check on company credit cards to see if he might be using them, and I found receipts for a hotel and restaurant in Seattle. I called our Bellevue office and left a message for them to contact you."

Quint interrupted, "Excuse me, but could I have the name of the hotel in Seattle?"

The secretary looked to Lai for permission. When he nodded, she answered, "The hotel is the Sheraton Regency; it is near our Bellevue office, sir."

Quint smiled, "That's very helpful, thank you."

Lai asked, "Is there anything else you would like to ask before she leaves?"

Then Quint indicated that he needed nothing more, Lai addressed the woman, "Very good. When you return to your desk, cancel Mr. Chen's company credit line, and call the hotel to let them know we will not be honoring his charges after today's date. When you return to your desk, continue trying to reach the Seattle office and find out if Chen reported in there. Please close the door on your way out and see that we are not disturbed."

The woman bowed, softly closing the door as she left.

"She is very thorough as you can see." Chong Lai held up the papers and said, "Permit me a moment to read this to determine what I can learn."

He read in silence until he finished. Quint watched as he frowned in concentration. His displeasure was apparent. Laying the papers on his desk, he said, "If you read Mandarin, I am happy to share them with you."

"I do not. Buster, can you read Mandarin?"

"A little, but not well. Mostly I just speak some Mandarin."

Quint shook his head, "We don't need to see them; however, if you could have an original copy and a translated copy printed for Gerald Williams, the CIA Director, that would be great. We understand if there is some confidential company information you do not wish to divulge." Quint handed him a card containing the address of the local Embassy which would be responsible for arranging a courier to hand carry the information to Washington.

"That is not a problem. There are no company secrets in this file. It is primarily Mr. Chen's work history and assignments with us. We will do an internal audit of this man's on-line work, any sites he has visited, the North Korean connection you mentioned, and any other information that is relevant, and we will provide the CIA with that as well. I would also request a written document of the events you have described to give to our authorities along with any substantiating information, for example your fiancée's tracking information that ties Chen Dai to the attacks. If Mr. Chen is returned here we will need them for prosecution. I suspect not only our governments, but Japan, and North Korea will also be interested in this."

"I suppose that will be up to our President and yours to determine who prosecutes."

"Naturally." Lai rose to signal the end of the meeting. "Do you gentlemen have accommodations here? If not, please allow me to arrange something."

"We appreciate your generous offer, but we are expected in Dalian as soon as we finish here. It has been a real pleasure to meet you, sir. I have been in awe of your accomplishments since I first read about you years ago."

"It is too bad you are pressed for time as I would have loved to arrange a tour of our facilities here. I am proud to say we are on the cutting edge of emerging technologies in the areas of artificial intelligence, robotics, and self-driving or autonomous vehicles."

"My fiancée would be thrilled at the opportunity to tour your company, and I would enjoy it, too. Should we be in Peking, I would love to take you up on the offer. Thank you for everything. You made our job here so much easier than I feared. Now, our mutual concern is finding Mr. Chen."

"I will coordinate with you if we locate him. Please let me know, if you find him first."

"Absolutely."

Again, the three men shook hands. Lai walked them to his office door and buzzed it open.

Quint and Buster exited the office to climb back into a taxi to make the return trip to the airport and the flight to Dalian. Again, Gerald had arranged CIA transportation allowing them to bypass the main terminal. By the time they reached Dalian and took the taxi to the CIA complex, both men were hungry and exhausted. Neither man was in any mood to conduct an interview with the North Korean escapee being held at the complex. The only thing they wanted was to check in and arrange for dinner before collapsing into bed. They were expected so checking in proved to be no problem and an on-site staff provided a meal which was delivered to their rooms within thirty minutes of their arrival. Buster brought his tray over to Quint's room and both men settled down in front of the television to catch up on the news piped in from the international CNN network. The steak, baked potato, salad, rolls, apple pie, and a good Chianti were soon history.

Buster leaned back in his chair and rubbed his belly, "Man, they sure know how to eat around here."

"Yeah, it was good. I guess these guys deserve some kind of compensation for doing duty here." Quint looked down at his watch and calculated the time difference. He figured no matter the time, there were two calls he needed to make.

Buster saw him checking his watch and nodded, "Gerald is going to want an update PDQ. You call, put it on speaker, and I'll listen in. There's not much for me to add since you were the one that conducted the meeting with Chong Lai."

Gerald picked up on the second ring. With the President pushing for answers, he was under pressure to resolve the situation before anything else happened.

Quint filled him in on what he had learned in Futenma, the second attack, and the information gleaned from both airmen and the radar technician. He continued with his visit to Baiduru and what he had learned, and what the CEO, Chong, would be forwarding to the CIA. He confirmed that the Baiduru company was unaware that Chen had flown to Seattle.

Gerald listened for twenty minutes without interruption, before asking, "So, in your estimation, there is absolutely no reason to assume Baiduru was in on any of the attacks?"

"None. I would swear that this hacker is some kind of lone wolf nut-job. I sure would like to know what he is doing in the States before he creates anymore problems. After the son of a bitch wrecked Lila, I'd hate to think he would go after her again. Plus, he created havoc in Asia, and we don't need it in the States."

"The Seattle CIA office and the local FBI are already on alert. Now that we know he checked into the Sheraton Regency in Bellevue we know where to begin looking. When we checked with the Baiduru Bellevue office, they were unaware of him even being in Seattle and had no email chain requesting him to come to their office. Since that is the case, we don't know if he will actually show up there or if this is just a temporary stop before he flies to another destination." Gerald paused, before asking,

"Have you had a chance to interview the North Korean our guys are holding in Dalian?"

Quint felt momentary guilt. "Not yet. I know you want this ASAP, but we were tired, hungry, and in need of sleep. We will get on it first thing in the morning and get back to you with anything we learn. Besides, the man was wounded escaping from North Korea and is on meds. They told me he already went to bed. I couldn't see getting him up for what could be hours of grilling. I want to be fresh and I want him to be, too."

"I suspect you are right, but for God's sake, get on it first thing tomorrow and if you learn anything important call me no matter what time it is."

"We'll do it."

After he hung up with Gerald, Buster returned to his room. After a shower, Quint climbed into bed and called Lila. He needed to hear her voice. He also wanted to warn her that the hacker was in the States. Perhaps, he could persuade Gerald to send another guard or two to Figure Eight to further secure things there. He would not mention that to her until it was arranged as he did not want to alarm her unnecessarily after all she had been through.

Chapter 17

Chen Dai had just finished his morning shower when he heard a soft knock on his door. Wrapping his damp towel around his body, he walked to the door and asked, "Yes?"

Feng Li whispered, "Dai, it's me. Open the door. I need to talk to you."

The moment he turned the lock and opened the door she pushed her way into the room and quickly closed the door in her wake. He could tell by her face that something was wrong. "What is it? You look scared silly?"

She gasped, "I am scared. Maybe, you should be, too. I just got a call from your company office saying that we are not to honor any of your charges beginning today. On top of that the CIA just showed up downstairs asking for you. I told them I saw you leave, and I don't know when you will return but that you probably went to your company office. They wanted to know how I knew you so well that I would recognize you, and I told them you have stayed here before and we talked, so that's how I know you. After all, I said, both Mr. Chen and I are Chinese. They left me alone, but they are sitting in the lobby bar waiting for you to come back."

"The CIA…yes, I know of them."

"Dai, they are serious trouble. They don't let up once they are after someone and they are after you. I'm terrified I will be fired for allowing you to check in without a reservation when we were totally booked. I didn't tell you, but I dropped another reservation to get this room for you. Since the Baiduru Company is a big client I figured I could cover myself. Now that they refuse to honor your charges, I don't know. Please, you need to leave now."

Dai turned his back and walked to the window. Pulling back the drapes he allowed the sunlight to wash the room in golden hues. He needed time to think. He could only assume that the bitch that was tracking him had nailed him once again. What she had done to put the CIA on his tail he did not know, but there was no way he could stick around to find out. He had to go to ground and fast. Feng Li was his best chance. He forced a loving expression onto his face, "My sweet Li, you are too beautiful to have such needless worries. I am sure there is some misunderstanding. Until I can straighten it out, I need your help. Can you get me out the service entrance and give me the keys to your apartment until I can find somewhere else to stay?"

She looked at him with indecision. Just because they had enjoyed a night of sex, she didn't know how far she wanted to go to help him. "Dai, if you have done something wrong, I don't want to get involved any more than I already am. Please, just go. I'll help you leave, but I am afraid to do anything more."

"I told you, Li. I have done nothing wrong. It is just a misunderstanding. Just let me stay at your place until I can contact my company and find out what is going on. You know what kind of paranoia people have against China. It is probably some bureaucrat that wants to make Chinese people look bad."

Her lips puckered in a pout. After several moments, she replied, "I told you I can't afford to get in trouble. It is all I can do to pay my bills now. If I lose my job, I am ruined. They will fire me if they find out I helped you, knowing you are being hunted by the CIA. What if they make me take some kind of lie detector test?"

Dai clamped down on his temper. He wanted to hit her and take the damn key, and if he knew where her key was, he well might have. However, that wasn't the way to play this. He needed a place to hide and time to determine what to do next. He forced his voice to be soft and cajoling, "Sweetheart, you are a silly, beautiful woman. I've done nothing wrong. You are not going to be in any trouble. I adore you and would never cause you problems. I promise. Now give me the key to your apartment so I can get out of here."

She dropped her head and shrugged her shoulders, "You promise?"

He pulled her into a hug and whispered, "I promise sweetheart. Now give me the key and I will leave."

She stammered, "I have to go downstairs. It is in my purse in my locker."

"Good girl, get the key, and when you return, I will be dressed and packed. You can show me the way out. I'll go to your apartment, and when you come home tonight, everything should be worked out. Alright?"

She nodded her head and ducked out the door, looked both ways in the hall to assure that no one had seen her and scurried to the stairs. She chided herself for falling for Dai, but from the first time he had stayed at the hotel, she had been drawn to him. It wasn't that he was the best-looking man she had ever seen, but there was something about him that appealed. He wasn't unattractive, but primarily she liked the way he projected confidence and a certain arrogance that drew her. Plus the sex with him was terrific. But, did she trust him? That she didn't know. However, she was giving him the keys to her apartment, and she had agreed to help him. Secretly, she could not help but wish that he might fall for her. With his self-proclaimed expertise with computer technology that he repeatedly bragged about, surely he could take her into a better life. She hated the dead-end job behind the check-in desk. She envisioned a future with a professional husband, children, a nice home, and being a stay at home mom married to a successful man who could give her the niceties of life. So far, Dai was the closest to fitting the image of the man she sought. At least, the side that he had shown her... Was there another? The idea of CIA agents waiting in the lobby was unsettling. Why did they want to question him and why had Baiduru put an end to his ability to stay at the hotel? Putting those troubling questions from her mind, she scurried to her locker, retrieved her purse, and fished out the key to her apartment. For a moment she held it in her closed fist against her chest. If she gave it to him, she was committed. Taking a deep breath, she nodded once and with a determined stride, walked towards the stairs. In five minutes, she was back at Dai's room door. Again she knocked, and waited for him to let her in.

She handed him the key. Without a word, he pulled her into a passionate embrace. When the kiss ended, Li felt much more reassured. This was meant to be. This was the man for her, so of course she would help him. His bags were packed, and he was dressed in a nondescript pair of jeans and a navy hoodie. Again she glanced both ways when they entered the hall. Motioning him forward, she led the way to the stairs. Once at ground level, the service hallway led them to a rear exit. Dai kissed her and told her he would see her after work and walked quickly away. At the corner, he turned and gave her a thumbs-up. Li returned to her position at the front desk where she would spend the remainder of the day looking at the clock slowly crawl towards the end of her shift. She smiled as she pictured Dai waiting for her. They would go out for a nice dinner with a good wine and afterwards, return to her bed and make love. She felt her arousal as she pictured the night to come.

Dai walked the short distance to her apartment and let himself into the small third story flat. He looked around the drab living room furnished with secondhand finds: the tiny bedroom, the bath with peeling wallpaper, and the miniscule kitchen with enough room for only one person at the time. Obviously not everyone in the States lived like royalty. The apartment was clean and neat despite an apparent lack of wealth. A small bouquet of fresh flowers on the coffee table added a cheerful note as did colorful posters advertising art shows. He put his bag in the corner of the living area, and decided to explore. He did not consider it nosy or rude. He was in survival mode, and anything he could use to help him escape, he would use. When he reached under the bed and pulled out a shoe box, he chuckled. Inside were several hundred dollars, no doubt Li's savings account. He took the money and put it in his wallet before sliding the box back under the bed.

Dai returned to the small kitchen table wedged into a corner of the living room and set up his computer. He did not have Li's server pass-code, so he tethered to his cell phone and logged in. In minutes he was on the server at Baiduru and accessing his account there. He started erasing anything that pointed to non-company activities and his contacts with Pong Ju and the incidents he had created. He had only erased a small portion of the file when the site stopped responding and the screen went blank. Cursing, Dai tried to get back in, but the server refused to recognize him. He swore under his breath. Now what to do? If he could not destroy those files, they could track his log-ins and trace him to the incidents with the North Koreans, Chinese, Japanese, and Americans. Without that log, there was nothing they could prove that would tie him to those events. He broke out in a cold sweat. After repeated tries at logging on, he got a ping telling him he was being tracked. He spent the next two hours doggedly pursuing whoever was after him: Baiduru, the CIA, or the one that had first nailed him...the woman in North Carolina? He typed furiously backtracking to the source of the ping.

"Ah, so you are up to your same old tricks. I thought I had killed you, you bitch. You started this entire mess, and I intend to see to it you pay. I think before I try to get to Iran, I have another order of business. I need to get you off my back...and this time for good." He was still talking to himself when he heard Li's voice at the door asking him to open it for her.

Dai shut down his computer and walked to the door. "Are you alone?"

"Yes, please let me in. We need to talk." He could hear the barely controlled panic in her voice.

He unlocked the door and she nearly stumbled in her haste to get inside. Once in, she leaned back against the closed door and took a deep breath. "You can't stay. I don't know why the CIA is after you, but if I keep lying, they can arrest me for not telling the truth. They told me."

"Who told you?"

"The CIA. They came back to my desk just before my shift

ended and started asking questions again. They spoke to my manager, and he checked the records for when you checked in and saw that I had cancelled another customer and given you the room instead. He is furious with me. I tried to tell him that I did it because the Baiduru Company is such a good client. At any rate, he told the agents what I did. They wanted to know if I'm your friend and if not why I gave you the room. I told them the same thing I told the manager. They acted like they don't believe me."

Dai studied her for a moment, before asking with deadly calm, "So, what are you planning to do?"

"I just want you to leave. I can't keep lying. I have to tell them that we are friends, sort of. Maybe, they will leave me alone then and not ask any more questions."

"Maybe, and maybe not." Dai took a deep breath. "I need to use your computer. Give me your pass-code so I can log on as you. I need to access something that I can't do from my computer. Don't worry it is nothing that will come back on you. As soon as I take care of some business, we'll grab a bite of dinner and when we get back, I'll collect my things and leave."

"I am sorry, Dai. I wish I could do more to help you but it is just too risky. I hope you understand?"

"Perfectly. Now let's have the pass-code."

Coming to a reluctant decision, Li gave him the code and went to the bathroom to freshen up while he logged on and did whatever was so important to do. She didn't ask and didn't want to know. That was one less thing she could answer if and when they questioned her again.

When she came back to the living room, Dai was shutting down her computer. He looked up and smiled. "Let's have something to eat here. It's probably better I wait until dark to go out just in case an agent followed you home. Do you have something you can cook?"

"It's not much. I have eggs, bacon, and bread. Will that be enough?"

"Perfect, then we'll have a last snuggle before I go. It may be awhile before I can return to Seattle." Dai smiled at her blush. He continued smiling to himself as he watched her scurry around the kitchen making a hasty meal. He was hungry, and he didn't know when he would eat, or have sex again. He intended to take whatever she could provide of both before he left. Her computer, charging cables, and cell phone were on the list. He would also go through her wallet for credit cards. He felt no guilt or compassion for what he had to do to Li. Her usefulness was almost at an end.

During the meal, Li chatted nervously. Dai only half listened, his mind too busy planning his next moves to take part in her attempted conversation. Finally, she fell silent. When he had eaten, she arose from the table and took their plates to the sink.

"Don't wash them now. Let's go to bed first."

He stood up and walked to the bedroom peeling off his clothes as he went. He trusted her to follow. If she didn't, he would still have sex with her before he left…with her cooperation or without. The idea of her putting up a fight wasn't unappealing. It wasn't necessary. Li came into the bedroom where he was already in bed, and slowly removed her clothing. When she was naked, she sat on the bed with her back to him. He reached up and pulled her down, ignoring the tears that ran down her face. He took her then, quickly and without waiting to arouse her. When he was finished and she was lying there with eyes screwed tightly shut, Dai put his pillow over her face and pressed down until she no longer struggled. Throwing the pillow to one side, he cursed at the sting of the claw marks she had left on his hands and arms. As he arose from the bed, he looked down at the wounds. Several were oozing blood. Walking into the bathroom, he washed up, and patted dry being careful not to get blood on the towel. He put his clothes back on without glancing at Li's limp body.

He returned to the living room, undid his suitcase and crammed both his laptop and Li's into it along with her charger, cables, and cell phone. He then went through her wallet removing her credit cards and the eighty-five dollars in cash. Glancing around the apartment, he checked to make sure that all traces of him were removed. He was ready to walk out the door when he remembered the dishes. Putting his bag down, he went to the kitchen sink and washed the utensils he had used leaving Li's untouched.

Satisfied that he had taken care of everything, he let himself out the door. Dai congratulated his foresight in using her computer to send an email to the hotel saying that due to sickness in the family, she would not be coming in to work for the next week or so. That should give him at least a week's head start before anyone came looking for her. She would be telling nothing more to the CIA.

Chapter 18

Quint requested breakfast for Buster and him to be served in his room at 8:00. His phone alarm went off at 7:30 and he was showered and thumbing through his notes when Buster knocked on his door. Almost immediately afterwards room service arrived with breakfast. Both men tucked into the American style breakfast of eggs, pancakes with maple syrup, sausage, orange juice, and coffee. Pushing their empty trays to one side on the table, Quint opened his folder, and he and Buster began reviewing the questions that Gerald Williams had provided. By 9:00 both men were ready for the interview. They intended to waste no time as they were booked on the 1:00 flight to Seattle.

They walked down the corridor from their rooms to the interview room that they had been told to use. Standing at the door was a tall, rugged looking man who introduced himself as Donald Compton. Buster and Quint introduced themselves and followed him into a small grey conference room…walls grey, chairs grey, table grey, carpet grey…both men looked at the grim room with distaste.

Buster declared, "Looks like you fellows don't much like color around here. This is about the damned most boring room I ever saw."

Compton laughed, "Don't tell me Director Williams sent an interior designer for the interview."

Quint grinned at Buster's discomfort. "Nope, Buster here has his own firm. He deals with sensitive issues for The Company. If you ever want a good man to have your back, he's the one. As for this room, I agree with Buster."

"Yeah, it is pretty sad." Compton motioned them to take two of the three chairs on the far side of the table. "As soon as I call Mr. Pah in, I will be joining you for the interrogation. Before you say anything, those are my orders as I have to determine whether or not he flies out of here in CIA custody, or we kick him back to the Chinese who will return him to North Korea. Furthermore, you don't speak Korean, and he doesn't know much English, so Director Williams asked me to translate. Personally, I think the man has something you are going to want to hear. He didn't say much, but he did indicate he knows something about that mysterious bombing of Futenma. I suspect that may be just the tip of the iceberg. He's nervous as hell, so we need to try to put him at ease first. He is fully aware we are his best hope. If he gets sent back, he's a dead man."

Five minutes later, Compton returned with a short, neatly dressed Asian with a shaving nick on his chin. The man was visibly shaking. He looked around the room before allowing his eyes to come to rest on Quint and Buster. Both men stood and motioned him to be seated in the chair across from them. Compton came to their side of the table and made introductions. After all were seated, Compton began, "Pah Pong Ju, these men are here representing the American government in Washington. They are going to ask you some questions, and it is very important that you answer them honestly. Take your time and think about your answers if you need to so you don't forget anything that might be important. They don't speak Korean, so

I'm going to translate. Why don't you begin by telling us why you left North Korea and why you think we should send you to the U.S."

Pah studied his clasped hands for a moment before beginning to speak. He was going to tell everything he knew no matter how damning. They would not believe him otherwise. Initially his voice was soft and shaking, but as he went on it became stronger and less hesitant. He described to them his father's death, followed by his mother's suicide. His hatred for the current regime was obvious, but he stated it anyway. He told about meeting a Chinese man called Chen Dai who worked for the Baiduru Company and said he was an expert in computer technology. Pah stuttered a little when he described that he was approached by Chen Dai and that he told him he wanted to cause problems for the North Koreans. He was careful to explain that he did not want anyone to be harmed, his only reason for working with Chen was to cause problems and embarrassment for the Kim Jong Un regime, and hopefully, cause it to fail."

Quint pursed his lips and studied Pah before stating, "I have two questions, Mr. Pah. First, tell me why this Chen fellow would want to help you hurt North Korea. Second, tell me how you hoped to accomplish this."

Quint's eyes held the North Korean's as Compton translated. When he was finished, Pah replied, "I never knew why he wanted to help me try to bring down the regime. I think maybe he's arrogant and power hungry. He thinks he is smarter than everyone else and this is a way to prove it. Somehow, I don't think he cares who gets hurt or what countries he damages. As for how he planned to do it, I wasn't sure. He asked me for information on North Korea's shipping near Pyongyang first. He wanted to create an incident, so I gave him the information on a ferry that was supposed to have few people on it. I did not know it had children on a field trip, or I would never have given him the information. He made it crash, and the children died. I have shamed my ancestors with this. I wanted to stop, but he wouldn't let me. He said if I tried, he would report me to my government, and I would be killed. What could I do? I didn't want to die."

Pah hung his head as he waited for the translation into English. Buster, Quint, and Compton exchanged glances. Quint made notes on his pad before continuing, "Mr. Pah, when he told you that you could not stop, what did you do next?"

After a moment, Pah looked up and took a deep breath, "He wanted the coordinates for missile test launches. I didn't have that information, so I talked to someone I knew…got him drunk, and he gave me what Chen Dai wanted to know. The man was my friend. He's dead now. I think Dai is responsible." Pah Pong Ju shook his head, "No, I know he is."

Again Buster and Quint waited for the translation. This time it was Buster who asked, "What did Dai do with the information this man gave him?"

"He made a missile land on a village in Japan. He also made one land on the American base in Futenma, not once but twice."

Turning to Quint, Compton exclaimed in English, "Holy crap, the Director gave me no idea why he was so eager for you guys to lead the interview. Now I understand."

"We've had suspicions but nothing solid to go on that would link Chen to any of the incidents."

Quint studied Pah Pong Ju. He seemed to be calmer and thus even more credible in the things he was relating. "Do you know if he had any way of causing a plane to go off course and nearly crash into a Chinese helicopter?'

"Yes. I think he was responsible for that as well, although neither my friend in North Korea nor I could have known the coordinates for U.S. or Chinese aircraft. He was working with autonomous navigation systems, and he knows how to hack into almost anything he wants. I think he put some kind of virus into GPS satellites. That's how he made the ferry crash and the missiles to go off course. My friend and I made it easier for him by giving the coordinates in North Korea. He must have hacked into the American ship on his own. Chen Dai says he is the best in the world…that no one is as good as he is at that sort of thing. You must believe me when I say he is really dangerous."

Quint waited for Compton to translate before saying, "Mr. Pah, did he have an ax to grind against the Baiduru Company?"

"I don't know, but I think he was just using the technology available at Baiduru to do these things. I don't think it had anything to do with getting even with Baiduru. I know he didn't think they appreciated him the way he thought they should, but he seemed to shrug that off."

Quint continued, "Do you know why Dai would want to cause an incident to harm his own country?"

Pah shook his head. His eyes were troubled when he replied, "No, I don't know him well enough to say, but I think he doesn't have any allegiance beyond himself. He's ruthless, evil. He has no conscience. Killing means nothing to him. I had to be free of him. I could not live with what he was making me do. My father's spirit rests uneasy because I bring shame on him and my ancestors."

Again Compton translated. Quint thought for a moment before continuing, "When you fled your country, were you running from your government or were you running because you were afraid of Dai?"

Pah sat straighter in his chair, "I am afraid of both. You see, my country already suspects me because my father was against this regime. Therefore, I carry the stigma of my father's sins against Kim Jong Un and his father. As for Chen Dai, he threatened me if I stopped helping him. He would kill me just like he did my friend. He doesn't care who he hurts. When I stopped answering his text messages, I realized it was only a matter of time before he either reported me to the authorities, or he came after me in some other way. No matter what he chose to do, I was dead if I stayed."

Quint stared at the grey wall above Pong Ju's head before asking, "If we needed you to do it, do you think you could get back in touch with Chen?"

Pah sat up in alarm. His voice was shrill when he replied, "He will kill me..."

Compton interrupted, "No, we can protect you. I don't know what the CIA will want to do with this and how you can help us track him; however, we are going to see to it that you are safely tucked away in the States."

Quint looked at Compton in surprise. He had assumed that Pah would be going to the States with them. "What was that?"

Compton stated, "Gentleman, this man is going to be on the plane smoking to D.C. The Director told me that if he gave you any helpful information to bring him in. I believe what we have heard this morning qualifies. He will be in my custody, and I'll make sure he gets there safely. Those are my orders. Director Williams didn't want to waste time flying the man with you to Seattle and then arranging transport to Washington."

"Fine, that makes things easier for us," Quint replied as Buster nodded agreement.

Compton stood, signaling the end of the meeting. "Is there anything else you need to ask before I take him back to his room?"

"No, I think we're done. I'll call Director Williams and let him know what we learned and that you are evacuating him as per orders. As for us, we are off to Seattle. It seems this Dai fellow did a runner, and Gerald assigned us to hunt him down."

"Shit. I sure as hell hope you catch him. He sounds like one bad hombre."

"Yeah, we believe he tried to kill my fiancée. You might say I have a personal stake in taking him out."

Quint and Buster returned to their rooms to pick up luggage. Quint called Gerald to report before he left his room at the CIA compound. He could hear the relief in the Director's voice that he could now go to the President with information that would get China off of his back. The Senators calling for retaliation against North Korea for the attack on Futenma would have to stop rattling their swords and find something else for the focus of their wrath.

Gerald told them the local agents in Seattle had lost contact with the woman they were questioning at the hotel and thought she and Chen might have gone to ground somewhere. Gerald also told him Lila had locked onto Chen, but he caught the intrusion and immediately blocked it. She was still after him, but until she could get another credible lead, it was a waiting game. Gerald was in a hurry to get them back to the States and running down Chen Dai as soon as Lila gave them a heads-up where he was or where he might be headed.

After hanging up with Gerald, Quint called Lila. He tried to keep the worry from his voice, when he told her what they had learned from Pah. Lila listened to the story without interruption. When he finished, she said, "Quint, I think he must be the North Korean connection I picked up on when I hacked into Chen's Baiduru computer. We could use him for bait maybe."

"I think that is Gerald's plan. In the meantime, you and Teresa need to be especially careful. This man has reason to come after you big-time. You need to do practice drills getting to the safe-room in case he shows up there. I also asked Gerald to send another couple of agents down there until we know you're in the clear and under no potential threat. He thinks the ones you have are enough."

"I should be okay. After all, Chen doesn't know I left Raleigh to come to Figure Eight."

"He found you in Raleigh by back tracking your hack. That means if he wants to he can track you to your location again. I'm not there to keep you safe, so don't be brave and cocky. This is one mean man. He has already murdered dozens that he had no grudge against like he does you. Remember, he already tried to kill you once."

"Crap. Now you've scared me."

"Good. Be careful. I love you too much to lose you to this madman. You promised to marry me and I'm holding you to it."

"I love you, too. I miss you, Quint. Hurry home and let's elope."

"How could I resist that offer?"

Quint left his room with a silly grin on his face. Buster immediately began teasing him about developing a crush on Gerald. Quint was too happy at being married in the near future to even respond. He decided to let Buster's curiosity gnaw at him.

In an hour Quint and Buster were sitting in the airport lounge of the private terminal where a government-chartered plane waited to carry them to Seattle. As they were walking to the plane, Buster commented, "Here we go again. Another plane, no clean clothes, more dirty socks and underwear, and not enough sleep. When I get finished with this job, Gerald is going to purely have a stroke when I turn in my bill."

"Man, if we nail this asshole, he's going to wine and dine you, plus pay your bill with a smile. Hell, I should be working with you instead of the government. All I'll get is an atta-boy and my regular government check."

"Not my fault, I have asked you to come work for me at least three times, you know."

"Yeah, yeah. Let's get our asses on this plane and back to the good ole USA."

Chapter 19

Pa Pong Ju's amazement at the prosperity and modern structures in China turned to open mouthed incredulity when he arrived in Washington, D.C. and observed the thousands of vehicles, the prosperously dressed people, and the imposing edifices that greeted him at every turn. He sat agape as Compton drove him to the safe-house where he would be lodged by the CIA for the foreseeable future. He prayed that he would be allowed to stay in this country. The very air in his lungs felt freer, buoyant…as though lifting him to a brighter future than he had ever dreamed possible. The old hatred that led him to want retaliation against the North Korean regime was being supplanted by a seed of happiness at his changed circumstances. Despite his abandonment of the Fatherland, surely his ancestors were smiling on him in this new country. His interview at the CIA by the man they called the Director assured him that he was a valuable asset… not just with his help in the anticipated capture of Chen Dai, but potentially in future operations. Despite not keeping in close touch, he had valuable knowledge of his father's surviving allies and other important dissidents in Korea. Furthermore, he had firsthand knowledge of the culture and inherent problems within the structure of the country. That unique connection was valuable in terms of providing information that might prove to be a factor in future relations between North Korea and the States. Even if his contributions to the CIA were limited in scope to the Chen Dai issue, he was reassured by the governmental men that he met that his permanent residency in the U.S. would be expedited. Even citizenship was an achievable goal. Compton's temporary residence in the safe-house as his watchdog did nothing to squelch his optimism. Indeed, North Korea did not yet know to where he had fled. If they learned his new location, Compton assured him that they could not touch him with the legal asylum granted him by the U.S.

Dai was another issue. He was both evil and vindictive, sociopathic and egomaniacal. If Chen Dai knew that Pah was helping the CIA in their effort to locate him and then by arranging some kind of meeting so the CIA could nab him, he would become Dai's enemy. At that point Pah's life would be immediately endangered especially if Dai continued to elude the CIA. Fortunately, Dai had no way of knowing Pah's current location and circumstance. Pah Pong Ju fervently hoped that would remain the case.

After settling into his temporary residence, he wandered around admiring the furnishings and modern appliances. Everywhere his eyes lit, he walked over to caress the object. The large refrigerator and pantry, both stocked with more food than he had ever before seen at one time, were enthralling. He had never dreamed a television could be as large as the one on the wall of the living area. Cabinets filled with every kind of dishes, eating utensils, and pots left him stunned. The size of the rooms, the quality and comfort of the furniture were equally unimaginable in his past life. He knew he was grinning like an idiot but could not stop himself.

For several minutes Compton watched him with quiet amusement. "Well, Pah, I think maybe you like it here?"

"It is more wonderful than my best dreams. Nothing in my life prepared me for this. Our dictator said such things are just Western propaganda. No one in Korea can conceive of such luxury when so many are dead of starvation and so many of the living have so little. You cannot imagine the contrast." Switching to the smattering of English he had learned, he continued, "Thank to you for help me to come here. I much appreciate."

"You are welcome, Pah."

"I amaze. Everything big here. People tall, big. Television big like movie. Refrigerator big, much food. My refrigerator in Korea small, not much food. Cars big. Room in house big. All big, nice, nice. I like."

"That's good, Pah. Now, let's see if we can earn our keep."

Pah was puzzled by Compton's response in English. He understood only the first part, not the second. "Again in English," he said. "I not understand 'earn our keep.' What this mean?"

Compton switched to Korean, "It means we work now."

Happy to relapse into Korean, Pong Ju agreed, "Yes, we'll work now. We must catch Chen Dai."

Compton nodded, "Exactly."

The men entered the study where two linked computers awaited them. Logging on, Compton directed Pah to attempt to connect with Chen Dai. Pah nodded in understanding, trying first the e-mail address for Chen at Baiduru. After several tries, he shrugged. "His computer link at Baiduru doesn't work."

"We did not tell you, but Baiduru blocked his access to their servers. They have been informed of what he is suspected of doing. We also did not want to alarm you before, but he is in the States."

"No! Why did he come here?" Pah was visibly shaken.

"Calm down, you're safe. I promise. As for why he came here, we are unsure. We think that when you did not take his attempted emails and calls, he thought you had turned him in to the authorities, so he fled from China. His company has an office in Seattle. He went there, but they blocked him before he got to their offices and they shut down his computer access to the Baiduru system. He must be furious. We have a very good tracker on his tail right now, but she has been unable to locate him after Seattle. She's still trying. We're hoping that is where you can help us. If you can contact him through another email address, then we can again try to track him. However, until he goes on line and we find his current location, he could be anywhere. Do you have another way of contacting him?"

"I have his cell number, also the email address of his personal computer. I can try both."

"Good. See if you can get him to respond to a call first. If he answers, keep him on as long as you can so our folks can try to track him. I will tell you what to say. If he doesn't answer leave a message saying you are trying to reach him with new coordinates he can use. If that doesn't work, we will try to send an email to his home computer."

"What do I say if he answers?"

"Tell him you have new Korean missile coordinates he can use that your friend gave you before he died. Tell him you still want to work with him. Say you stopped responding because you were scared and needed time to think."

"And if he asks for those coordinates, what do I say?"

"I will write them down for you. Whatever you do, do not tell him that you left North Korea. This computer you are on has been routed through a series of servers to your old address, so he will have to do a lot of digging to blow your cover. If he trusts you, he will have no reason to do that."

"I understand. I will try to call now. My phone is not so good, but we can hope."

Pah rang Dai's number and waited for him to answer. His hands were wet with perspiration. Switching the phone to his left hand, he wiped his right palm on his pants before transferring it back. After ten rings, Dai's voice came stating he was away from his phone and to leave a message. Pah left the instructed message and ended the connection.

Compton smiled and did a thumbs-up. He wasted no time calling Gerald to alert him that Pah had made contact, and they were awaiting a response. Gerald called both Lila and Quint. Lila was to try to establish a location using CIA protocol to backtrack his phone and computer depending on which he used to make contact. Quint and Buster were on alert to relocate as soon as Lila determined Chen Dai's location.

Compton leaned back in his desk chair, and looking over at Pong Ju, stated, "Good. Now all we can do is wait."

Five minutes later, the computer the CIA had programmed to look like Pah's old address pinged to signal an incoming email. Compton sat up in his chair. "This is it. Let's see what he's got to say."

Compton leaned over Pah Pong Ju's shoulder as he read the message that Chen had sent. The man did not appear suspicious, merely directing Pong Ju to send him the new missile coordinates. He also warned Pong Ju not to call his phone again. Instead he gave a new number, one that Compton immediately recognized as a Seattle number judging by the area code. Chen further ordered Pong Ju not to call him at his new number unless it was an emergency. The email address he gave was not one of Dai's previously used addresses, leading Compton to surmise that either Chen Dai had stolen or borrowed someone's phone and computer, or he had enrolled for new internet and cellular phone service in the Seattle area. Either way, it was a place to begin searching for the man. Pong Ju typed in the coordinates that the CIA provided and looked up to Compton for approval before sending the email and signing off.

Lila was already hard at work attempting to trace the email address Chen used to its origin in the States. Gerald had agents investigating the phone Chen used to call to determine if it was his or he was using someone else's. In a matter of hours, they had discovered the phone number belonged to Feng Li, an employee of the hotel in Seattle where Chen Dai had registered. The two agents, who had talked to Miss Feng earlier, returned to the hotel to ask her why Chen Dai was using her phone and computer connections. When they asked at the front desk to speak to her, the man on duty pointed them to the manager, Merv Andrews. Andrews, a short stocky, balding man with a sour expression, informed them that she had called in two days prior with a family emergency and would be away from work for several days, leaving him short staffed. In a matter of minutes, he provided them the address he had on file for Feng Li.

Thirty minutes later, the agents arrived at her door, knocked, and stood in the hall glancing around at the dingy surroundings while they waited. When she didn't answer, they looked one another in the eye. The taller and older of the two men, Lester Lowery, LL to those who knew him, spoke, "I think the lady's not home. So either we get a search warrant which could take some time, or we get creative."

His sidekick, Bobby Winters, made a wry face. "Come on, LL. How many times are we going to get written up for breaking the rules, before they kick our balls to the curb? Three more years you can retire, Bud."

"Yeah, but that's three years away and this is here and now." LL fished in his pocket and came up with a slender piece of metal which he inserted into the door. The odor hit them the minute they entered the living area. Pulling handkerchiefs from their pockets, they walked into the small bedroom. They did not need to get any closer to know she was dead. Without touching anything, they backed out and returned to the hall outside the apartment. Calling the Washington CIA office, they asked to speak to the Director for further instructions. Following Gerald William's directions, they immediately phoned forensics to get over ASAP and then began securing the crime scene. Once they had donned gloves, the first order of business was to check for any signs of intrusion. Seeing none, they then examined her body for wounds. There were no obvious injuries to indicate how she had died. Next, they slipped plastic bags on her hands to preserve any possible evidence. LL lifted the bed sheet. Li's body was nude beneath it. He pointed to a dried track of what appeared to be semen on her right thigh. "Looks like she had sex just before she died. I suspect, since there are no visible wounds, she must have been smothered to death."

Bobby nodded, "I'm going to start checking for a cell phone, laptop or computer."

"While you are at it, find her purse and see if you can determine whether or not it was riffled. I'll finish up in here and look around the bathroom while we wait for the coroner and the others to arrive."

"Will do."

"Holler if you find anything."

Five minutes later, Bobby called him into the living room. "I checked everywhere and I can't find a phone or computer. Her purse is here, but the wallet has been emptied out…any cash or credit cards are gone. I looked in the kitchen, and it appears she ate a meal and left the dishes in the sink. There is only one set there, so she may have eaten alone."

"Or, whoever killed her washed up to destroy evidence he was here. My hunch is this Chen Dai character is the perp since Director Williams says they intercepted a call from him on her cell phone. Once we date the time of death, if the call dates to that time then he made it from here. If not, he's on the run. I don't think he'll be coming back here at any rate. I looked around the bedroom and bath, but there is nothing to indicate anyone was living with her…no men's clothes or toiletries. I didn't find anything to indicate she had a steady boyfriend. We'll poke around at work and see if she was dating. It's possible a jealous boyfriend might have killed her."

"Yeah, we gotta tick every box. Sure looks like this Dai character is the one though."

The sound of sirens brought their reflection to an end. Both men stepped into the hall to await the others. The coroner was the first to appear at the top of the steps, followed closely by the forensics team. The new arrivals listened intently while LL described what they had found. Once they were fully filled in and LL had stressed the critical nature of the investigation, as well as the need for careful haste, the two agents left it to them to continue mopping up the crime scene.

Returning to the Sheraton, they again asked for the Mr.

Andrews. LL had to stop himself from laughing at the expression on the man's face. He guessed the two of them were about as welcome as a case of STD. Grinning despite himself, LL asked for a private meeting to gather information. Andrews wasted no time getting them out of the public area and into a private conference room where their presence could not alarm any of the hotel guests. They spent an hour with him but learned little.

Next, they began questioning any of Li's co-workers that were on duty. They systematically interviewed each employee on every shift until all had been questioned for any small shred of information about her private life and any connection to Chen Dai. It was not until the following day, that they got their first lead from another front desk girl, Linda Norris, who had been off the previous day. According to Norris, Li had no steady boyfriend. Li had hinted that she had dated a Chinese businessman that worked for the Baiduru Company when he was in town, and she seemed to really like him. Norris also gave them the name of Li's parents. She didn't know the address, but with the resources available to them, the agents had that in a matter of hours.

The next stop to visit her parents, and tell them of their daughter's death, was not one they relished. The insensitivity of the questions they would be forced to ask grieving parents was not lost on either man.

Chapter 20

Quint was worried. Chen Dai had not used the coordinates Pah Pong Ju gave him. Nor was he using the Feng woman's phone or computer. Without some way to track him, they were helpless. Furthermore, he was disgusted with sitting around in a hotel room with Buster in endless speculation about where the man was headed.

On the other side of the continent, Lila was frustrated that she was stymied in her own effort to locate Chen. She had discovered nothing since the man had used Feng Li's credit card to rent a car in downtown Seattle. He could be anywhere. They had only three ways to locate Chen Dai: the phone, the computer, or a credit card charge. So far, apart from renting the car, he had used none of Li's cards. Presumably, whether Chen was traveling or was staying in the Seattle area, he was using cash for gas, food, hotels. As long as he did that and maintained silence on both phone and computer, all they could do was hope that he made a mistake. The longer they stayed in the dark, the more worried Quint became. His calls were getting on Lila's nerves even though she understood that he was thinking of her safety with Chen on the loose.

After calling Lila for the third time in so many hours, Quint called Gerald to say he wanted to return to Wilmington and let Buster stay in Seattle waiting for the next clue to Chen's intentions, but Gerald told him to stay put in no uncertain terms.

Trying every rationale he could come up with to rebut the directive, he ended the call in suppressed anger when none of his arguments worked.

The entire thing went against his gut feeling. Long since he had learned the hard way to trust his gut. If he defied a direct order, he incurred the wrath of not only the CIA, but the President who was being kept fully informed of every detail. If he stayed in Seattle, he could not protect Lila if Chen was out to kill her for disrupting his carefully orchestrated plans. He did not know the man. He did not know what he was thinking or planning, but he hated to ignore the fact that Lila could be a target. Sure, she had the safe room and a couple of government agents to protect her, but he wanted to be with her if Chen showed up. Even knowing how well trained and thorough the agents Gerald sent to Figure Eight were, it was one of those times when he trusted no one else as much as himself to get it right if she were endangered by Chen. He knew the safety systems he had installed. Even though he had told the agents at Figure Eight where and how to activate them, he did not trust them to have such ingrained knowledge that they could intuitively use them in a crisis. He tried to console himself that he was overreacting due to an emotional involvement, but it did not reach the unease in his gut. He talked for an hour with Buster who was as frustrated as he was even without the same personal relationship with Lila, a probable target should Chen Dai be moving east.

Buster just plain hated to sit still and wait on anything. He was a shoot first and ask questions later kind of guy. Quint was not. He was more analytical and unemotional in most situations. This was not most situations. This was about the woman he loved.

Quint had good reason to worry.

*****

Chen Dai was busy trusting his own gut. Something about the call and email from Pah Pong Ju did not ring true. Chen Dai had pondered for hours as to why he would be contacted by Pong Ju after days of silence. He quickly realized the email with new coordinates, except for slight modifications, was a repetition of something the man had already given him. Chen sat in a rest area on the outskirts of Seattle for two hours researching the modified coordinates before he determined they were bogus. Chen could only surmise that someone had gotten to Pah Pong Ju and convinced him to cooperate in order to incriminate him. How stupid did they think he was that he could not see through such a sham? When Chen Dai had the information he was after, he got out of the rental car and used the rest area toilet. While inside, he collected brochures for hotels along the route east. Returning to the car, he counted his cash and that which he had stolen from Li. He then figured an amount for each of his basic expenses: gas, food lodging. When the money was depleted, he would have to risk stealing another wallet or purse. As long as he did not use phone, computer, or credit cards, those who chased him would not know where he was or where he was heading. He laughed at their arrogance in thinking they could outsmart him.

Another thought occurred to him; was there a tracking device in the rental car? He dismantled the on-board tracking system. He sat thinking for a moment before fishing around in his pocket for his knife. He used it to remove the license plate from the rental and then walked to a nearby car and switched plates. In a few more days, he hoped to be where he wanted to be without worrying about being tracked.

Once he connected with Interstate 90 going east, he breathed a sigh of relief. What he would do on reaching a final destination, he had not yet figured out. The first thing he had to do was get as far from Seattle as he could. He had no way of knowing if Li's body had been discovered and whether or not her murder could be tied to him. If that should happen, he wanted to be lost in this huge country.

As a foreign national, there was no chance he could purchase a firearm, and without any experience, he would be afraid of using one even if he were able to buy a gun. But, he wasn't too concerned. There are many ways to kill someone. Feng Li was the first he had killed in direct contact with his victim. The other killings were incidental and remotely accomplished through the activation of computer algorithms. Li's was a personal murder, a sometimes friend and lover. He had far more reason to feel some remorse for her killing than the one that now claimed his focus, yet he felt nothing. It was as easy for him as squashing a bug under his shoe. Li had been useful, but when she could no longer serve his needs, she became a threat and thus was expendable. Pah deserved killing for turning on him. That could wait; at the moment he had other priorities. His next target deserved his animosity and killing. The logistics of how he would accomplish his immediate objective would be determined when he arrived and had time to assess the location. He had an address, but that worried him. He had noted no activity from that location in weeks. When he checked into his hotel that evening, he would start fishing to see if his nemesis had changed locations and IP address. If so, he would find it.

By the time he reached Rapid City, he was exhausted. His limited driving experience and the speed of American cars on the interstate highway had resulted in several close calls. Added to that was the constant need to interpret highway signs and directions…all written in a language very foreign to his own. His eyes were tired. His brain was tired. His entire body was tired. And, he was hungry. Prior to checking into the Econo-Lodge Motel he had spotted just inside city limits, he drove to the nearest café…a small diner advertising a meal for $5.00. He wasn't expecting much, and he was not disappointed. The plate the harried waitress slapped on the dirty counter contained an unpalatable and overcooked piece of meat and vegetables boiled so long they were nearly gray. He was too hungry to care. On the stool beside him was a young man who spent his entire time studiously texting. Just as Chen Dai finished paying for his meal, the man stood and headed in the direction of the toilet leaving his phone on the counter.

Chen had pocketed it and was in his car before the young man returned and realized his phone was gone. In minutes Chen Dai was parked behind the Econo-Lodge well out of street view. In five minutes, he had removed the phone tracer app, changed the timeout settings, and created a new password. With that done, he checked into the hotel. Once in his room, he tethered Li's computer to the man's phone and changed the settings on Li's phone to those of the one he had stolen to disguise the IP address. Using his new phone's navigation app would make the next leg of his journey to Gary, Indiana much easier. When he reached Gary, he hoped he would again get lucky. Even if he did not, he would trash the stolen phone keeping the Sim card for potential use.

Chen took a quick shower before crawling into the lumpy bed and pulling up the covers. A neon sign just outside his room that shone through his thin drapes in intermittent flashes was irritating but not enough to keep him awake. The next thing he knew the room phone was chiming a wake-up call. He turned on the television and waited for the news to see if there was any report of a murder in Seattle. When nothing was mentioned, he did not know if that was because Li's body had not been found, or news from Seattle would not normally be reported all the way from there to Iowa. Chen Dai turned off the TV. Groaning he arose, shaved, and dressed before throwing his things back in his bag and leaving the hotel. His only stop that day was to gas up, use the service station bathroom, and grab some snacks from the counter when he paid for the tank of fuel.

Once he reached Gary, Indiana, he again checked into a cheap hotel and asked at the desk for directions to an inexpensive restaurant. The thought of a dinner like the one the previous evening was enough to make his stomach rebel. He decided he could afford a reasonably priced meal. The restaurant the desk clerk recommended was close to the hotel. Once he was seated, he looked around at the nearby tables. At the closest one, a woman had dropped her handbag on the floor by her chair. Her coat, draped carelessly over the back, spilled over the edge of the bag and was close to his chair. If he was careful, Chen thought he might be able to ease his hand down and retrieve her wallet without being noticed.

Once his meal was delivered, the waiter had left, and he had eaten, Chen again glanced around the dimly lit room. No one was paying him any attention, and the woman and her male companion appeared to have eyes for no one else. Casually he dropped his napkin on the floor next to the bag. In seconds he had lifted the flap, reached in, and extracted the wallet. Concealing it in his napkin, he sat back up and signaled the waiter for his tab. Leaving the correct change and a small tip, he exited the restaurant and drove back to the hotel. He did not check the wallet contents until he returned to his room.

He ignored the credit cards. They were useless as the woman would report the wallet stolen, and the authorities would know where and how if anyone attempted to use the cards. He would not leave that trail. Cash was another matter. In the bill section of the wallet he found over $300 dollars in cash. That was enough for gas, hotel, and meals from Gary to his final destination if he was careful. He chuckled to himself. So far, he had used only $25 dollars of his own money. Pleased with his cunning, he had a good night's sleep and was on I65 south early the next morning. According to his map he would then take I70 east from Indianapolis. He planned to spend the final night before arrival at his destination in Charleston, West Virginia.

When he checked into his hotel in Charleston, Chen tethered his phone to the one he had stolen and began an internet search of his Dropbox records. It was essential before continuing from West Virginia to determine his exact destination. He could not afford mistakes. He hoped it would not be in the CIA's backyard. After over three hours of fruitlessly combing through old files saved from when he had uncovered his initial tracker and downloaded her contacts, he found a clue. Acting on a hunch, he began searching a new name, Quinton Cord. Chen wondered how Cord tied into the series of events that had brought him to his current predicament, or if it was a wild goose chase that would lead him nowhere. After another five hours, he still was unsure how the new information tied in. Too exhausted to even log out, he fell asleep with his phone in the bed beside him. He overslept the next morning. It was nearly time to check out before he was dressed and ready to leave. He still had no clear idea of where to go next. Fearful of using his own phones to continue searching, he walked to the motel office and asked if they could direct him to a nearby internet café. When the desk clerk saw his confusion at the verbal directions, she carefully drew Chen a map. The café was less than a mile away.

For the next six hours, he searched leads. Leaning back in the uncomfortable plastic and chrome chair, he stretched in relief. He had his destination. Walking to the counter, he paid his bill ignoring the attendant's curiosity and desire to chat. He walked out the door and looked around. He did not see a likely place for a meal. After eating nothing since the night before, he was starving and too tired to drive as far as he had hoped to travel that day. He got back into his car and turned onto the interstate. Several exits down, Chen saw signs advertising food and lodging. He would eat and spend the night before driving the final leg of his journey.

Chapter 21

Quint held the phone from his ear and flinched when Gerald hung up with a bang. He sheepishly glanced over at Buster and shrugged.

Buster laughed, "I could see that coming. I gather our friend Gerald ain't none too happy with you about now. Hell, I don't know if I am. It's no fun sitting here feeling useless, and it will be worse all by myself. But, man, if I were you, I would be out of here, too."

"Yeah, I know. This sitting around here feels all wrong. Dammit, Chen could be anywhere. Hell, he's had enough time to be in Wilmington by now. As long as he lays low, spends cash, and doesn't use his phone or computer, we will stay in the dark as to what the devil he's up to. If Gerald wants to fire me, let him do it and to hell with this job. I have enough I don't need the government's damned money. That's not why I was doing this in the first place and Gerald knows it." Quint swiped his hands through his hair making it look like a messy pile of hay. "Fuck. I hate going against him."

"Simmer down. You don't need to tell me." Buster pointed to the packed bag standing by the door. "Take your stuff and get your tail on that plane home. Call me when you get there. If I learn anything here, I'll let you know."

"Thanks, Buster. I owe you one for covering things without me." Quint picked up his bag, and turning at the door, gave

Buster a thumbs-up.

Buster grinned and waved, "Good luck. You keep that woman of yours safe."

Quint nodded and was gone. The Uber car he had called was waiting at the curb when he walked out. Directing the man to take him to the Delta terminal at the airport, he sat back in his seat and fidgeted with the briefcase he held in his lap. The adrenalin was still pumping into his bloodstream following the call to Gerald. The usually stoic Director had lost it when he told him he was flying home against orders. He hated he had angered Gerald. The man was not only his boss but his friend. He tried to explain he had no choice, but Gerald wasn't buying it. The Director had quickly reminded him that three of the CIA's best operatives were in Quint's home to protect Lila. 'What in the hell did he think he could do that the other agents couldn't?' Gerald had demanded. Intellectually he admitted to himself, that they were as good at their jobs as he was or Gerald would not have sent them. The difference was Lila was just an assignment to them. Sure, they took it seriously and would do everything possible to protect her if she were threatened in any way, but he was the one that loved her and wanted to be with her should Chen Dai again try to kill her for tracking him and leading to his exposure. He fished his phone from his pocket and called Lila to tell her he was on the way. The airport was in sight when he ended the call. Now if the damned plane would just be on time.

He was booked on the 12:24 non-stop flight to RDU. It was scheduled to arrive in Raleigh at 8:26 p.m.. He figured by the time he collected his luggage, caught an Uber car to his house on Park St. to pick up the spare car he kept in the garage there, and drove to Wilmington it would be midnight.

On arrival at the departure terminal, Quint tipped the driver and collected his bags. The line at the Delta counter wasn't long nor was the special security line his CIA credentials allowed him to use. Once past security, he grabbed a newspaper, some snacks, and walked to the boarding gate. He glanced at his phone. He had mere minutes to spare. Not bothering to wait with the bored looking crowd that was sitting at the gate, he stood near first class check-in. Being one of the first on would not get him there any faster, but it made him feel better.

Once in the air, he put his seat back and closed his eyes, but troubled thoughts made him restless, and he could not sleep. He broke out in a cold sweat at the thought that Chen Dai could already be in Wilmington and plotting to kill Lila. It was a relief when the plane touched down and moved slowly down the tarmac to the arrival gate. In minutes, he had his luggage and was in an Uber on his way to his Raleigh house.

On arrival, he disarmed the heavily secured residence and walked into his bedroom where he gathered a few clothes. From there he made his way via the hidden staircase to his office where he stored various weapons. He did not know what he might need but he planned to be prepared. On a whim, he walked over to his desk and flipped on the footage for his security cameras. In seconds the entire perimeter of his house was displayed on the screens. Quickly he scrolled through the last twenty-four hours to see if anyone had been at the house. He almost missed the image on the far-left screen. Scrolling back, he replayed the footage. Glancing at the time on the screen, he noted that a man's image appeared between 6:23 and 6:31 PM. Quint replayed the screen several times as he studied the furtive figure that was walking around the house. He then checked the other cameras and found the same figure on them in that time slot. Despite repeated replays, he could not get a clear facial image. It could have been anyone, but he strongly suspected Chen Dai had arrived before him. He wished the man had tried to break into his home rather than just circling around it. If he had, he would have been in for some of the nasty surprises Quint had rigged for intruders. As it was, he could only wonder why Chen bothered to come to Raleigh and then move on. Was he even now outside and watching the house, or had he learned that Lila was at Quint's home on Figure Eight? Either way, he could afford to waste no time when Chen had nearly a three-hour head start.

Swearing under his breath, he called Lila and warned her to go to the safe room with Teresa and to alert the agents on duty. He then called Gerald. Not reaching him, he left a message on his phone. Quint then left his office and ascended by another hidden staircase into the garage where his spare car, a recent model 530 BMW, sat with a full tank of gas. Activating a hidden panel on the wall that gave access into the back street, he drove out between concealing shrubs, closed the sliding wall, reactivated his security systems, and made his way to the Beltline. In fifteen minutes, he was on the interstate to Wilmington.

The two-hour drive to his home on Figure Eight Island had never seemed so long. Despite driving far faster than the speed limit allowed, he felt as though he would never arrive. The only time he moderated his speed was when his Escort warned of a radar signal from a patrol car. The minute the Escort stopped chirping he pressed down on the pedal to regain his previous speed. He could smell the adrenalin inspired scent of his perspiration. He had always hated that odor, but for once his conscious mind barely acknowledged it. His entire focus was arriving on the island before Chen Dai.

When he drove over the bridge onto the island, he reached for the semi-automatic pistol he kept secured in a holster attached to the dash, and put it in his lap where he flicked off the safety. On the passenger seat were various other weapons he had created. One was a small missile-carrying drone. There were several flares also on drones that were designed to light up the grounds around his home. In a small leather bag on the passenger side floor were several military-issue grenades, along with the strongest canisters of pepper spray yet devised. In cases on the floor behind the front seat lay an arsenal of weapons including a loaded 50 caliber AK-47 assault rifle. He shuddered to think what the highway patrol would have done if he had been stopped for speeding. As it was, he looked like a one-man army right down to the Kevlar vest he had buckled on at the last minute prior to leaving Raleigh. Once on the island, he drove to a block from his house, pulled to the side, and stopped the car in the sandy edge.

Quint opened his door and listened to the sounds of night on the island. The soft murmur of waves along the shore, wind in the rustling palms and low growing pines, and the noise of night creatures were all as it should be. To prevent the agents guarding the house from shooting him, he texted them that he had arrived and was coming in. Next, he texted Lila, and Gerald to notify them he was there. Even though it might annoy some of the neighbors, he activated the drones carrying flood lights and sent them on a path programmed to circle the perimeter of his grounds and the shoreline. Motion activated lights would immediately pop on should an intruder get beyond the outer edge of the lawn. He next sent up the missile-carrying drone which was programmed to circle the lawn harmlessly unless he signaled it to fire. He inserted his pistol into a hip holster. Picking up the bag of grenades and pepper spray, he slung it over his left shoulder before hefting his sniper rifle. He hoped he would not need to use the heavy assault weapons and left them behind. Locking the car, he crept into the bushes along the road and began a cautious approach to his house. When he reached the brightly drone-lit perimeter of his own property, he squatted in the bushes and again listened for anything out of the ordinary. Shielding his phone screen, he texted the agents requesting them to report in. Neither agent responded. They had to have seen the drone spotlights on the outer edge of the property and along the beach, so why were they not acknowledging him. Cursing softly, he dialed their number and held his breath as he waited for them to answer. Again, he got no response. His nerve endings were firing overtime. Something was off. After killing the spotlights on the drone, he used his phone access to deactivate the motion sensor lights around the property. If Chen was out there the darkness would protect him, but it also prevented Quint from being shot by the agents, or being spotted by Chen.

He skirted the yard hugging the dark shadows from the surrounding shrubs. At the closest point to the guest house, he ran at top speed towards the shadows at the end of the building. Quint flattened himself against the wall and took several calming breaths. When his breathing and pulse were back to normal, he started inching around the cottage. He had not gone more than six feet when he was grabbed from behind in a hammer lock around his neck.

The man growled in a low voice, "Identify yourself and you better make it good or I'll break your damned neck."

"Kirk, Kirk Young, is that you?" Whispering, Quint used his

hand to ease the pressure on his neck. "I'm Quint. I tried to call you a minute ago to let you know I'm here."

Kirk released him, "Sorry, Quint. I'm really pissed. I just found the two other agents. One was by the hedge over there and the other at the back door. They're dead. Looks like they were jumped and then garroted with a wire. Whoever killed them took their guns. I didn't answer the phone because I didn't want to give away my location. That is one mean son-of-a-bitch out there."

"Are Lila and Teresa locked in the safe room?"

"Yeah. They should be safe for now. We couldn't get Code to go with them. I don't know where he is. He barked about five minutes ago and I've heard nothing since."

"Crap." Quint sent up a silent prayer that his dog was okay before signaling Kirk, "You take the right side and I'll take the other. You armed?"

"A Luger."

"Take a couple of my grenades, too. Try not to blow up my house if you can help it."

"Got it. Watch your back."

"You, too."

Quint flipped the safety off of his pistol and started moving to the left. The tricky part would be the covered archway between the guest cottage and the main house. The arch-posts provided some coverage for anyone hiding there, whereas he would be fully exposed until he could gain the passage connecting the two buildings. Just as Quint crouched and prepared to run, he felt something cold nuzzle his hand. Quint hissed, "Good grief, Code, you about scared me to death."

Code grabbed Quint's pants leg and pulled trying to get him

to back up. Trusting his dog, he stepped back into the shadows just as a bullet zinged harmlessly past. Catching the flame from the gun when it fired, he knew the man was in the arched passage way. Kirk should also have noted the direction of the gunfire and hopefully was closing in from behind. If they could get the intruder in a cross fire, they would have him. Digging out his phone, Quint programmed one of the drones to fly under the archway and light it up.

When light flooded the passage way he could see the man's shadow from where he huddled behind one of the arch supports. Kirk pinged his phone to let him know he had the man in his gunsight. For a moment Quint was tempted to shoot it out and kill him on the spot, but Gerald had given specific orders, that if at all possible, to take Chen alive. Keeping that in mind, Quint hollered, "Chen Dai, we know who you are. You are surrounded. If you want to live, toss out those guns and come out with your hands in the air. If you don't come out by the count of ten, you're a dead man."

Quint paused a moment and then began to count: "One… two…three…four…five…six…seven…eight. You're pushing your luck Chen, now toss out those damned guns or on ten, you're fucking dead. Nine…"

"No, wait." One gun was tossed out, shortly followed by the second pistol Chen had taken from the two dead agents.

"That's good. Now walk out slowly with your hands in the air."

Aiming his gun at Chen's heart, Quint studied him for several seconds before growling, "I really want to kill you, asshole. But it seems the government wants you alive. Now, face down on the ground and put your hands behind your back."

Kirk walked out of the shadows, "I have him. I'll get my cuffs on him and I'll call Gerald to let him know we have him and that I've got two agents down."

Quint waited until Chen Dai was in cuffs before asking, "Can you handle this, Kirk?"

"No problem. He gives me any trouble I'll shoot him in both kneecaps."

"Works for me. While you finish up here, I want to let Lila and Teresa out of the safe room. Let me know if you need anything."

"Will do."

Quint leaned down and scratched Code behind his ears, "Thanks, buddy. You are a good friend."

Code gave a bark and nodded his head in agreement. Following his master, they walked into the main house and made their way to Quint's bedroom. There he pressed the lever to a hidden panel that slid open to reveal two women sitting on the sofa inside playing a hand of cards.

Both Teresa and Lila threw down their cards and glanced up in alarm. Lila cried, "Oh, my God. Thank goodness it's you." Jumping up, she ran to him.

Quint's arms closed around her, and he hugged her into a tight hug. "I am so glad I got here in time. We have Chen under arrest. He's never going to hurt you again."

Lila looked into his eyes and smiled, "Oh, Babe, I have been so worried about you. I am just so happy you are home."

"So am I." Quint tore his gaze from her to look at the other woman, "Teresa, you doing okay?"

"No, problem. Let me out of here and I'll go cook us up a celebration dinner for the three of us and those agents."

"Only one agent now. The other two didn't make it. I suspect

Kirk will be leaving with Chen Dai ASAP, so don't count on him either."

Lila groaned, "Oh, God, I don't even want to know what Chen Dai did to them, do I?"

Sadly, Quint shook his head, "No. We just have to be glad he'll not be killing anyone else."

The three of them left the safe room with Code in the lead. Kirk was waiting for them in the living room with Chen beside him. When Chen saw Lila he glared at her and opened his mouth as though to speak. Quint stared hard at him daring him to say anything. The others swung their focus between the two men as they waited to see what Chen would say. When he remained silent, Kirk tilted his head toward his captive, "Gerald wants me to take Chen to Washington. There's a plane waiting at the airport. He's going to use him to glean everything he can about this virus he implanted in those satellites. Once that's done, he's no use to us anymore. With both China and North Korea clamoring for him, I suspect his future is not going to be pleasant if he's ever out of U.S. government custody."

"What about the two dead agents?"

"Someone should be here in the hour to mop up the crime scene and take care of the bodies."

"Thank you, Kirk, for taking care of my people and Code here. And I am so sorry about your buddies. Let me know if their families need anything, and I will do what I can to help."

"Neither one was married, so it's just their parents. The government will cover all expenses for them, so don't worry. It's a damned shame they had to die, but that's always a danger in this game. We accept the danger when we sign up. I'm just glad it's over."

"So, am I." Lila piped up, "Now I can start planning a wedding."

"Why don't we just elope?" Quint murmured just before he started kissing her. Neither of them looked up as Code, with a deep growl, escorted the agent and Chen out the door.

Titles by Betty J. Vaughn

Previously her books *The Man in the Chimney* (first published as *Muddy Waters*) and *Turbulent Waters* (first published as *Blue Waters*) won the award for historical fiction from the North Carolina Society of Historians for 2011 and 2012 respectively. She is the 2013 winner for her book *Run, Cissy, Run*. The fourth book in the series, *The Intrepid Miss LaRoque*, won in 2015. The novel *Yesterday's Magnolia* is not part of the historical fiction series. *Tiger's Code*, a CIA thriller, is the first book in the Quint Cord series. *Dragon's Sword* is the second in the series. All seven books are published by Total Recall Press.

In honoring her books, in a unanimous decision, the judges commented: "It is gratifying to find an astute historian whose skills far exceed that realm; someone who can take facts and weave them together with fiction and end up with a story that actually could have happened...[It is] a wonderful story full of emotion, unexpected twists and turns, close calls and tragic moments...Mrs. Vaughn can consider herself a seasoned novelist...[Her books] are fast paced, action packed, and full of adventure...Her work simply isn't just a flurry of words, dry, and boring...She is a master of literary technique as she weaves her tapestry of words."

Fiction Award NC Society of Historians 2010 through 2015

NC Society of Historians
Established December 1941

AWARD WINNER

Judge's Comments:

"It feels like one is reading a living history rather than one fictitious by nature. The book is wonderfully written, and as the story unfolds, it is realistic in that it 'could' happen and probably did to many during the War Between the States, and it is exciting, heartbreaking, tense and relaxing.

Anybody interested in the War Between the States from a layman's view would enjoy reading this book. The story, which is difficult to chronicle in limited space, has been lovingly crafted by an author whose heart is in the South and whose soul is in her characters. Kudos for a job well-done. Kudos!"

Title: *Run Cissy Run*
- Betty J. vaughn
- Language: English
- Hard Cover Book ISBN: 9781590956748
- Paper Back Book ISBN: 9781590956755
- eBook / ePub: ISBN: 9781590956762

You would think Cecilia LaRoque has it all: a loving father, wealth, beauty, social position and a devoted suitor. She doesn't. Crushed by a cold and critical mother who soon absconds to live with a dissolute lover, 'Cissy' struggles to prove herself worthy of love and respect. She could not have foreseen in her teenage years that the genteel and privileged life she had led would come to a crashing halt with the outbreak of Civil War, a bitter struggle that would tear her world apart. Despite the hardships and inherent danger, she seizes the opportunity to forge an unorthodox role for herself as a spy.

Title: *The Man In The Chimney*

- Betty J. vaughn
- Language: English
- Hard Cover Book ISBN: 9781590956021
- Paper Back Book ISBN: 9781590956038
- eBook / ePub: ISBN: 9781590956045

The War Between the States has come to eastern North Carolina, bringing hardships, pillaging, and fear to the local residents. For those left at home, the struggle to procure the needs of daily life is all-consuming; for those serving in the armies of both North and South, death is a daily companion. Against this backdrop, an unlikely and forbidden love affair between a local woman and a Union officer leads to difficult choices for them both—choices that will tear them apart and force them to deal with the abandonment of their dream of a life together.

Despite broken hearts, misunderstandings, and missed chances, Penny and Ryan strive to survive the dangers and ravages of war and make the best of their separate futures. With the surrender of the South at Appomattox, Penny realizes she has one last chance to either find the man she loves or settle for a life alone.

Title: *Turbulent Waters*
- Betty J. vaughn
- Language: English
- Hard Cover Book ISBN: 9781590951743
- Paper Back Book ISBN: 9781590951750
- eBook / ePub: ISBN: 9781590951767

LOVE IS PERSONAL, WAR IS NOT, especially in North Carolina, 1865-1867, during the reconstruction. With a love they are certain will transcend all else, southern belle Penny Kennedy marries Union Officer and attorney, Ryan Madison, despite the condemnation of those around them. The initial days of wedded bliss end abruptly when Marcus, the man who courted Penny for years in anticipation that she would marry him, is arrested for murder, and Ryan is assigned to prosecute him. As hard as this development is to tolerate for Penny, she will discover worse things await her before Ryan and she can attain the life they desire.

Title: *The Intrepid Miss LaRoque*
- Betty J. vaughn
- Language: English
- Hard Cover Book ISBN: 9781590957103
- Paper Back Book ISBN: 9781590957110
- eBook / ePub:: ISBN: 9781590957127

When Wilmington falls in February of 1865, Cissy LaRoque no longer needs to spy. That will not stop her from finding a new career where she can prove her worth beyond societal expectations of a woman. With the war drawing to an end and Wilmington occupied, she is faced with desperate circumstances. Ryan Madison, a Union officer from the past, and Brandon McLean, a new one, attempt to help her. While attracted to them both, she is aware of family and community hostility toward the enemy and dares not act on the attraction. Her fiancé, Logan who is fighting for the southern cause, does not arouse her ardor like the two Union men. When the Confederacy falls, she convinces her father to allow her to run his shipping office in New Berne while he maintains the main office in Wilmington. There she discovers Ryan has married and Logan has jilted her. Provoked and titillated by a man she cannot have but craves, she puts aside romance and concentrates on business. Despite her father's initial objections, much to his surprise she succeeds far beyond any expectation. Although she is happy in what she has achieved, she is frustrated by what she has lost.

Title: *Yesterday's Magnolia*

- Betty J. vaughn
- Language: English
- Hard Cover Book ISBN: 9781590955543
- Paper Back Book ISBN: 9781590955550
- eBook / ePub: ISBN: 9781590955567

Jo envies Margo and Maurice for their ready charm, looks, wealth, glamour, and exciting lives never realizing that it is she who is envied for a life that contains the things that they themselves long for and have not attained.

"It's a shame to have so damned much and yet so little." An eastern North Carolina farmer's daughter, Margot, streaks like a comet into the life style of the rich and famous. Her beauty and exuberant, zestful personality gain her entrance to boardrooms, the White House, a corporate jet stocked with Cristal champagne and caviar, a villa in Italy, and marriage to one of the world's most powerful men. Maurice, the spurned suitor, seeks friendship and comfort from Margot's sister, Jo, a quiet, bookish art history teacher. Jo envies them both for their ready charm, looks, wealth, glamour, and exciting lives never realizing that it is she who is envied for a life that contains the things that they themselves have not attained. Like the comets they so resemble both Margot and Maurice are consumed by the friction of life, leaving Jo to remember the magic moments they brought to a more conventional path.

Title: *Tiger's Code*

- Betty J. vaughn
- Language: English
- Hard Cover Book ISBN: 9781590953907
- Paper Back Book ISBN: 9781590953914
- eBook / ePub: ISBN: 9781590953921

Quint Cord's latest assignment is proving to be his most challenging and could well lead to catastrophic events if he does not break the code in time to avert them.

Quint Cord is an unlikely spy. With sufficient family money so that he never needs to work, he could have spent his life idling on a beach chasing women. But from the moment he discovers famous codes of the past in a university class, he is hooked. His unique talent for creating and breaking codes brings him to the attention of the CIA.

A powerful and ambitious politician, who's in cahoots with a Saudi prince, plans to seize the US presidency and throw the western world into turmoil. Quint flees the country only to stay one step ahead of a foe determined to kill him before he can break the code.

Clue by clue, Quint begins to zero in on his target but can he stop him in time?